Ali Smith was born in Inverness, Scotland in 1962. Her book of short stories, *Free Love* (Virago 1995), won the Saltire First Book of the Year Award and a Scottish Arts Council Book Award. Her first novel, *Like* (Virago 1997), was nominated for the Saltire Award.

*f*ree love
and other stories

Ali Smith

A *Virago* book

Published by Virago Press 1998

First published by Virago Press 1995

First published in Great Britain by Virago Press Ltd 1995

A CIP catalogue record for this book is available from the British Library

ISBN 1 86049 584 2

Typeset in Perpetua by M Rules
Printed and bound in Great Britain by
Clays Ltd, St Ives plc

Virago
A Division of
Little, Brown and Company (UK)
Brettenham House
Lancaster Place
London WC2E 7EN

For Sarah, for Margaret,
for Hardy and for Wood

Acknowledgements and thanks are due to the following publications, where stories from this collection have already appeared:
Gairfish, HarperCollins Scottish Short Stories 1994, Scotland on Sunday, The Scotsman, Second Shift.

Contents

Free love

The first time I ever made love with anyone it was with a prostitute in Amsterdam. I was eighteen and her name was Suzi, I don't think she was much older than I was. I had been cycling round the town in a bad mood and had come upon the red light district quite by chance; it was the most pleasant red light district I've ever got lost in. The women there sit on chairs in windows that are lined with furs and fabrics, they sit breast naked or near naked, draped with gowns and furs. It took me a while to work out that they were probably scowling at me so contemptuously not just because I was staring but because I wasn't business.

It was evening and I'd been out cycling by myself. I had wandered down a back street and had stopped to put my jumper on, and my bike had fallen over and the chain had come off. It was when I stood the bike up against the wall of a building to get a proper go at the chain that I noticed the cards stuck by the door. Several of them were in English, one said Need To Relax? Take It Easy No Rush Ring Becky. Another said Dieter Gives Unbeatable Service Floor 2. Another said something about uniforms and domination and had a drawing of a schoolgirl on it. I was just laughing at them to myself when I saw one at the bottom in tiny writing and several languages, Dutch, French, German, English and something eastern, and the English line said Love for men also women, Suzi 3rd floor. The also was underlined.

That's when I left my bike standing and found myself going up the old staircase; on the third floor there was a door with the same card stuck on it and my hand was knocking on the door. I had a story ready in my head in case I wanted to get away, I was going to say I was lost and could she direct me back to the youth hostel. But she came to the door and she was so nice, I took to her at once and wasn't the least bit scared.

The flat had one room and a bathroom off it, some chairs and the bed and a hanging bead thing curtaining off the kitchen area like in photographs of the sixties. On the wall there was a poster of the lead singer from A-Ha, A-Ha were big at the time in Europe and she said she liked him because he was a man but he looked like a woman. I remember I thought that was a very exciting thing to say, I hadn't heard anyone say anything direct like that before. I come from a small town; one night my friend Jackie and I had been sitting in a pub and two girls had been sitting at a table on the other side of the room; they looked conventional, more so than we did really, they had long hair, were wearing a lot of make-up, and it was when I glanced to see what kind of footwear they had on that I noticed one of them had one foot out of her high-heeled shoe and was running it up and down the other one's shin under the table. This was a very brave thing to be doing now that I come to think about it; chances are if anyone had seen them they'd have been beaten up. At the time I pointed it out to Jackie and she said something about how disgusting it was, I think I even agreed, I never wanted to disagree with her on anything.

The prostitute spoke English with an American accent. She said she had an hour and would that be enough for me, and though I hadn't a clue I said yes I thought so. I showed her my hands all oily from the bike and said I should maybe wash them, and she sat me down in one of the old armchairs and, bringing a cloth and a washing-up bowl over, washed and dried them for me. Then she did this thing, she put my hand to her mouth and put her tongue between my fingers at the place where my fingers meet my hand, and she pushed it in, going along between each. I think my head almost blew off just at her doing that.

She gave me a cup of very strong coffee and a glass of red wine, she told me to help myself from the bottle of wine she left on the little table next to the chair, then she put her arms around my neck and kissed me, and loosened my clothes, and undid my jeans, and I sat there amazed. She took my hand and took me on to the bed, she didn't even pull the covers back,

3

we stayed on top, it was August, warm, and afterwards she showed me what to do back though I did have a pretty good idea. When eventually she looked at her watch and at me and smiled and shrugged her shoulders, we got dressed again and I took out my wallet and thumbed through the guilder, but she put her hand over mine and closed the wallet up. It's free, she said, the first time should always be free, and when she saw me to the door she said would I be in Amsterdam long and would I like to come back. I said I would very much like to, and went down the stairs in such a daze that when I came to my bike I got on it and tried to cycle it away, completely forgot about the chain and nearly hit my chin off the handlebars. So I pushed it back to the youth hostel and I felt as I walked past the reflections of the tall buildings curving in the leafy surfaces of the canals that life was wondrous, filled with possibility. I stopped there and leaned on the railings and watched the late sun hitting the water, shimmering apart and coming together again in the same movement, the same moment.

When I arrived back at the hostel Jackie put the chain back on for me. Jackie and I had been friends since school, she'd been in the year above me, and we'd stayed friends now we were both students. We'd saved our summer money to go on this trip. I'd been serving in the souvenir shop on the caravan site since the end of June and she'd been behind the bed and breakfast counter of the tourist information board; we made a pittance but it was enough to get us return tickets for a cheap overnight bus to Amsterdam.

Jackie was blonde and boyish and golden in those days. One day I had simply seen her, she was sitting on the school wall by

the main door and I had thought she looked like she was surrounded with yellow light, like she had been gently burnt all
over with a fine fire. At a party we'd sat in a dark corner and
Jackie had nudged my arm, her eyes directing me to a handsome thuggy boy lounging on the couch opposite watching us,
her mouth at my ear whispering the words, see him? Tonight I
only have to smile, you know, that's all I have to do.

I had thought this very impressive, and had held her head for
her later in the upstairs bathroom when she was being sick
after drinking a mixture of beer and wine; we sat on the stairs
laughing after that at the girl whose party it was going round
the living-room hoovering up other people's sick into one of
those small car hoovers; after that we had been friends. I don't
know why she liked me, I think because I was quiet and dark
and everybody thought I must be clever. I'd thought Jackie
was beautiful, I thought she looked like Jodie Foster on whom
I had had a crush, she looked like Jodie Foster only better. I'd
thought that when we were at school and I thought it then,
even though Jodie Foster's film career had hit rather a low
spot at the time.

I'd had these thoughts for years and they were getting harder
and harder to keep silent about. I didn't really have a choice.
Once we got to Amsterdam and she saw there were people
selling big lumps of hash in the street she was filled with moral
outrage, that's what she was like. But the overnight bus had
been a great excuse to lean my head on her shoulder, to have
my nose in her yellow hair and pretend I was asleep, which
meant I was very tired the first day we were in Amsterdam,
going round in a stupor telling myself it was worth it.

Already Jackie had made contact with a boy from Edinburgh whom we met in the youth hostel kitchen, his name was Alan; already they were big friends and he'd suggested she should go and watch him sword-fight at a tournament that night, which is why I cycled off in a terrible mood. I was in really rather a good mood by the time I came back to the hostel, and Jackie, who hadn't gone to the sword-fight after all, went into a sulk because I was happy for some reason and because when she asked me where I'd been I wouldn't tell her.

Nothing could spoil my holiday after that, I didn't care any more. And that's when Jackie started being unusually nice to me; this was confusing because although we were best friends we were pretty horrible to each other most of the time. The next day she hired a bike too and we cycled up and down by the canals and the crammed parked cars, we drank beer and ate ice cream under restaurant parasols, we visited the Van Gogh Museum and Rembrandt's House and the Rijksmuseum full of old Dutch paintings, we went to a shop where they made shoes while you watched. The day after, we cycled to a modern art gallery; downstairs they had a room sculpture where people were sitting round a bar and their faces were made of clocks. We wandered this gallery for a while and upstairs I lost Jackie and fell asleep on one of the wooden seats. When I woke up she was sitting very close to me, her arm on my shoulder. I sat up and she didn't move away; we sat there looking at the picture I'd fallen asleep in front of, it was a huge rectangle of red paint with one thin strip of blue paint down the left hand side. Her leg was pressing firmly into my leg. Do you like this? she asked, looking at the picture, and I said I did, and she suggested we should go and visit the Heineken factory now.

At the Heineken factory they give you a tour of where and how the beer is made, all the steps in its brewing process, how it's bottled, how the labels are stuck on and where it goes after that. At each stage they give you a generous glass of beer and everyone on the tour shouts cheers or *pröst* and drinks it. Then they take you into their office for after-tour drinks. By the time we'd done the Heineken tour we were so drunk we shouldn't have been cycling at all and had to leave the bikes against a tree and lie on our backs in a park, laughing at nothing and looking at the sky. It wasn't as if we'd never been drunk together before, but somehow this time it was different, and we sat in the grass in the late afternoon and I told her all the things I'd felt for years now, and she looked at me woundedly, as if I'd slapped her, and told me she felt exactly the same. Then she put her arms round me and kissed my mouth and my neck and shoulders, we were kissing in the middle of Amsterdam and nobody even noticing. Even after the Heineken wore off the afternoon didn't, it lasted for the rest of the holiday, me with my arm through hers on the street, at nights in the youth hostel dormitory Jackie reaching up from her bunk below mine to press her hand into my back, us holding hands between bunks in the dark in a room full of sleeping people. Very romantic. Amsterdam was very romantic. We took photos of each other at the fish market, I still have that photo somewhere. We went boating on a lake and took pictures of each other rowing.

The day before we were supposed to be leaving, on the

pretext of going out to do some mysterious present buying I cycled back to the red light district and left my bike at the bottom of the stairs again. I had to wait this time for half an hour. Suzi remembered me, I know for sure because afterwards she sat up, looked at her watch, smiled and ruffled my hair, saying, it's sad darling but the second time you have to pay. It was good, but not as good as the first, and it cost me a fortune. On top of which I had to buy Jackie a present; I remember it was expensive but I can't remember what it was I actually bought her. I think it was a ring.

Of course when we got home we stopped being able to do things like hold each other's arm in the street, though we did manage to snatch a little time after hours in the back gardens of unsuspecting people, in lanes and alleyways between houses or garages, in the back of her father's van parked in the dark by the river. Otherwise it was downstairs at either of our houses after everybody else had gone to bed, on the floor or on the couch, one of us with one hand over the other's mouth, both of us holding and catching our breath.

The first place we really made love was arriving back home after Amsterdam in the women's toilets at the bus station, hands inside clothes, pushed up against the wall and the locked door in the minutes before her father was due to come and take us and our rucksacks home. It was one of the most exciting things I have ever done in my life, though Jackie always called it our sordid first experience. About a month after, I walked past the tourist information board and saw through the window in the back office Jackie heavily kissing the boy who worked on the Caledonian Canal tourist boats. I thought that remarkably more sordid, I remember. But then, what people think is sordid is relative after all; the person who saw us holding hands between our seats at the theatre one night thought it sordid enough to tell our mothers about us in anonymous letters. We both had a lot of denying to do and that's something that certainly brought us closer together at the time. We had that to thank them for. Recently Jackie and I lived in the same city again for a while, and we were always nice to each other when we'd meet occasionally in the street. We both know we owe each other that, at least.

But I date the beginning of my first love from that August in Amsterdam, and we lasted over five years on and off before we let go. I think about it from time to time, and when I do the picture that comes first to mind is one of the sun as it breaks apart and coheres on the waters of an unknown city, and I'm there, free in the middle of it, high on its air and laughing to myself, a smile all over my face, my wallet in my pocket still full of clean new notes.

A story of folding and unfolding

My father sits on the bed in the bedroom at the back of their house, one hand just brushing on the raised ridges of the candlewick cover over the continental quilt, the other holding a pair of women's pants coloured a very light pink. The light is on in the room at four o'clock in the afternoon.

The room smells clear and airy, of something like talcum powder. There are fitted wardrobes that, if opened, reveal clothes neatly arranged with shoes jigsawed into pairs in the dark at the bottom. There are fitted cupboards, this one full of presents given by friends and children, some placed on one

11

side waiting for use, some stored on the other to be recycled usefully into presents for friends and other relatives. In another there are books of photographs, albums over forty years since the first one. Next to this cupboard there is a mirror, round which photographs of children are stuck, slipped in at the corners in the little gap between the mirror and its rim. There are bottles of perfume on the dressing-table in front of the mirror, and a pair of glasses, and leather gloves with the shapes of hands still in them. In one drawer are boxes of jewellery, little plastic boxes that say *Silvercraft* on the tops, with necklaces, brooches, rings nestling inside them on cotton wool strips; these boxes are, just in case, hidden under a magazine called *Annabel* dated New Year 1977. On the front of the magazine the year's horoscopes are promised.

Two bedside tables sit on either side of the double bed on which my father is sitting. One has a clock radio and a still tidied store of crime fiction and fishing books, the other has three small pillboxes that, when you open them, have separate compartments for different tablets. Beside these are medicine bottles and pill bottles made of plastic, different sizes arranged beside each other like the architectural model of some complicated building. Each table has its own lamp, and the one with the plastic bottles also has an electric blanket regulator next to the lamp.

In the chest of drawers two drawers hang open, one hangs lower than the other. In the middle one are brushes and combs, and a collection of lipsticks. This drawer smells pleasant, waxy and thick of make-up. The room has the air and the smell of someone who's just left, throwing the last lip-print paper tissue crushed into a ball into the tin wastepaper bin, her movement through the room displacing the settled air like a light breeze in humid weather, but it's winter, and the big light is on, the room is stark, and my father is sitting on the bed looking at his feet or the floor.

The pants resting in his hand are smooth, you can still see the crease from their having been ironed. In the chest of drawers, in the open drawer next to the one filled with lipsticks and brushes, there is women's underwear, and round my father on the bed is spread more, more pairs of Marks and Spencer's cotton ladies' briefs, smooth cotton coloured in pastels, blues and pinks, peach colours, in little haphazard spilling piles, clean, soft from having been worn and washed. My father's fingers are large and rough, the seams of his fingers look dark against the slightness of the pair of pants he holds; he is holding them as if he doesn't even know they're there. He is looking at his feet. The pants lie gently round him colouring the room so that he looks out of place, some country swain from a Thomas Hardy novel wooing someone he has no chance of having on a hillside of meadow flowers, offering one his clumsy hand has pulled up, not knowing the words to say it with.

In the open drawer are larger, longer pairs of white pants, made to offer more support to stomachs, made of a material that shines when the electric light catches it. My father looks up from the floor to the drawer, and turns to look at us, standing in the door-frame of the room. Then he looks around him at the scattered contents of the first drawer he's picked to unpack. What, he says. What am I supposed to do with all of this?

Twenty-five, after the war, after having pretended to be old enough to enlist in the Navy. After his bombed boat with the drowned bodies in it is taken into harbour in Canada, and they saw into the metal side of it and the bloated bodies gush out with the water; after recovering from his arms mysteriously stopping working, all the muscles refusing to respond. Just before his mother dies of cancer and just after the nightmares about the planes coming over start recurring, one of the electricians is larking about with his apprentice mate in the women's dormitory of the WAF station while the women are all elsewhere working. The electricians are wiring some lights up in the places men don't usually get into, and are high with excitement, high as boys at being let loose in with the beds and the imagined smells of women. The room is hardly exciting, it's a drab room filled with the air of punctuality. The beds are identical, identically made, sheet folded over blanket and pillow tucked under, regular and neat, tightly packed; each bed has a wooden chair and a knee-high locker next to it, and there is nobody supervising the men because today the electrician is in charge.

The lights have to be wired with cable which must be fitted next to the ceiling all the way along above one row of beds, and the electrician is teaching his apprentice how to fix cable tidily so it won't be noticed and so nothing can be hooked on to it to bring it down. He's holding the ladder steady while his apprentice nails the thin cable up along the top edge of the wall, where the wall meets the ceiling.

The ladder is positioned next to one of the first of the lockers in the row, and as his apprentice hammers, his head squashed sideways against the ceiling to do so, the electrician notices that the door of the locker isn't properly shut and so he gingerly coaxes it open with his shoe. The locker door clanks alarmingly loud, the apprentice shakes on the ladder, and the electrician steadies him and halts the door's swing with his foot, at the same time he checks behind him to see that nobody is coming into the dormitory. The two men grin at each other in delight.

Pictures are stuck all over the inside of the locker door; the electrician recognises a picture of Bogart sitting on the other side of a desk from Bacall. This one likes hers ugly, mate, he shouts up to the apprentice. On the shelves of the locker clothes are crammed; the electrician puts his hand in and, winking at his friend, runs his hand over the front of a hard-starched uniform shirt. From the top shelf he pulls a pair of greyed-white women's pants, and as his apprentice watches laughing he holds them up to his nose, raising his eyebrows and closing his eyes in mock intoxication, then leaving the pants covering his face and looking up blindly in the direction of the apprentice, he sings through them, le – t me put my arms about you, I – don't want to live without you.

Watch the ladder then, says his friend, laughing.

The electrician folds them back up, places them on top of the others, shuts the door and holds the ladder steady as the apprentice climbs down. The next locker along has clothes stuffed in any which way, and several pictures of Sinatra taped on to the inside door. Not so good, though she's got better taste, says the electrician. In this locker clean clothes have been mixed with dirty laundry, as he soon discovers when he plays the pants game again with some well-soiled pair.

Serves you right, says the apprentice, though it's a game he wants to play too, so with one eye on the door in case of interruptions, they work their way through an examination of the dirty and clean underwear, and move on to the next locker and the next, giving marks out of ten for the smell and the state of the contents.

But then the apprentice comes to one locker that's stuck, he can't open it with his fingers because the handle's off its door and the door's firmly wedged shut. There's a small hole in the metal where the handle was, however, and the electrician rummages in his overalls chest pocket and takes out his small screwdriver and, inserting it into the little screw-hole, jerks the door open. It swings back. A light scent escapes.

Oh, the apprentice breathes.

That's the best. That's the winner, says the electrician shaking his head. The few clothes in this locker are remarkable, not grey but white, and smooth, arranged and unrumpled, folded with talent. The underwear on the top shelf is thin and white. The electrician reaches in and feels his hand touch something silken. He pulls gently and a petticoat disarranges itself, coming away in his hand and knocking the underwear out of harmony as he takes it out and it falls away from his hand like liquid, like light. The two men watch it as it hangs, moving, unearthly and lovely. The electrician is struck by guilt, and by delicacy.

How in hell's name are you going to fold it up again? asks

16

the apprentice. The electrician memorises the name above the bed of this locker. Later in the week he will ask her out and find her as lovely as her underwear to him, and a little later still he will tell her about his mother dying, and, sitting in the pub one night he'll show her his mother's wedding-ring in its wooden box with the velvet inside. She'll say, oh yes, it's a very pretty ring, and as she says it someone at the next table will see the scene, misread it and shout out, they're getting engaged! They're getting engaged! and all of the people round them in the small pub will smile and point and jog the shoulders and arms of the couple looking at each other in laughing alarm and embarrassment, and the people at the back will try to see what's going on, to catch a glimpse of the ring, the couple, anything of the moments and materials of which love gets made.

Text for the day

Imagine Melissa's collection of books, spread between her bedroom and her living-room, when Melissa was in bed at night asleep or out at work all day or away for the night or weekend. Hundreds sitting silent on their shelves from Agee to Yevtushenko (she had no Zs). A substantial set of English and Scottish literature course canon classics – Melissa studied English at university ten years ago. A large collection of recent American, English and European literature; Melissa's friend Austen works in a bookshop and often lets her buy books at ⅓ discount. Books and books, blocks of books shifting infinitesimally in the night as the renovated tenement foundations sent shivers through the building. Books pressing together, so close that the covers of several of them stuck together; for instance if Melissa had tried to remove Charlotte Brontë's *Villette* (Penguin) to read again she would have found it attached on one side to *Shirley* (Penguin) and on the other to a 1933 copy of *Testament of Youth* by Vera Brittain (Gollancz), signed by the author and found for 50p in a public library sale.

Imagine the silent books in the silent flat at night, unmoving in the dark, Melissa's name, the place she bought them and the date shut in each between the first page and the outer cover; imagine the spines of the books by day in the still flat, yellowing, losing their colours, fading with the light moving round the room.

First of all Melissa told her boyfriend Frank to piss off and get out, she was fed up of him calling her Honey, it wasn't funny any more. And the next day instead of going to work she stayed in bed, pulling the covers up to her neck and, when the heating had gone off and it got cold, using her hairdryer to warm herself between the duvet and the mattress, something she had always refused to do before because of global warming and the electricity bill. After that she got up and threw her hairdryer out of the window; it smashed on the pavement just missing the next door neighbour's car. She threw all the windows open in the freezing cold. Then she threw her books all over her flat. That was then. Now she was fast disappearing, she was almost gone.

Later, when she had been gone for quite a long time, those who were less imaginative among the friends who noticed she wasn't there any more thought she was probably off doing something like taking time out, backpacking across the USA or something like that. Someone else, someone at work, thought that maybe she'd landed some hot new job better than Information Transference and had taken it without telling her old boss so she wouldn't have to work notice. Though neither of these was really like her, like what you'd expect. Other friends and acquaintances didn't notice or know, most didn't think of her at all and those who did assumed on the whole that she was still where they'd last seen her, doing what they'd last known she was doing, rather like you assume someone you know is doing the usual things, breathing, walking, going to the shops, eating biscuits, before you discover that he or she is dead, died a long time ago and you never knew it.

Austen knew something was wrong though because she had a key to Melissa's flat and the books, the books, the pride and joy, were so peculiar in both rooms, in such a mess, all over the floor or piled in haphazard order, great gaping holes in the bookcases all up the walls and books fallen on their sides askew, even a scatter of books in the bath. Like the advert on television showing a burgled house to warn you against thieves and suggest you leave your light on at night to pretend someone's always in, Austen thought. The light in Melissa's flat had been left on, baleful with the curtains and windows still open. Nobody there and nothing taken, everything smugly intact except the books.

21

She shut the windows in the cold and turned the heating on in the kitchen cupboard. On the table some loose-torn pages lay beyond a milk bottle; from where Austen stood she could see, distorted through the glass of the bottle, the word *Introduction*. By her foot, the cover of a Kafka paperback (Penguin Modern Classics). She made herself a cup of tea – sour milk – opened the pedal bin to drop the teabag in and found the bin was full of the ripped-out pages and the empty shell covers of several books. Down the back of the bin, more loose pages on the floor. She went through, sat on the couch and found her feet resting unavoidably on books. Beside her on the cushion, as if it had landed there clumsily after flight with its wings still fanned out, lay an upside-down copy of Seamus Heaney's *Seeing Things* (Faber and Faber).

Right then, as Austen dipped her finger into the tea to squash a lump of milk against the side of the cup, Melissa was leaving an eight till late supermarket in the rain, gnawing something out of a packet, a paperback in her other hand, and an elderly lady wearing a rainmate was shouting after her in a rare kind of anger, her arms in the air, calling to the boys collecting the trolleys in the wet carpark to look, look what the girl had done, never in all her life.

Frank phoned Austen the next evening. He didn't particularly like Austen, she was Melissa's friend.

—She told me to get out, Austen, so, well, ha ha, I *did*. She went a bit mad. I'm a bit worried about her, said Frank. He was still pleased with himself for having demonstrated to

Melissa how absurd her demand was by actually doing what she asked.

—Mm. Funny, I'm not, I don't think.

—Not what?

—Worried. At least I don't think so. Mad like what? Like when you spilt the hot chocolate on the Keats and all over the couch? said Austen.

—Well, no, not really, it wasn't mad-angry. It was because she was so calm, it was weird.

—Right, weird, said Austen.

—But that made it, you know, *more* mad. She said these really weird things just sitting on the floor, cool as a cucumber talking this stuff.

—Mm, said Austen. She didn't like Frank much, hadn't liked him since the first moment they met, when he had told her she had a weird name.

—She's not at the flat, you know, said Frank.

—I know. Look, Frank, I've got to go.

—Do you know where she is?

—No, I don't, but how about if she calls I'll tell her to call you. Look, I've got something frying on the cooker.

—I can't get an answer and I can't get into the flat any more. Nobody knows where she is at the office, she hasn't phoned in sick, I called to ask. Do you think I should tell the police?

—Well, no, not really, but if it'll make you feel any better, said Austen absentmindedly.

Later that evening Melissa phoned Austen and Frank from a callbox. It was a bad line and her voice was faint, from the middle of a sea of white noise.

—Austen, you shouldn't have tidied up. No, it was good of you, but — yes, I went to pick up some things. No, listen, I can't stop, I've only got twenty pence — listen — use the flat if you like. *Have* the flat if you like, enjoy it, and Austen, use the car. I'll send you — I don't know — a postcard (her voice grew fainter) must go —

—Hello Frank? It's me, Melissa. Oh Christ DON'T call me that — yes — no, can you hear? I am, as loud as I — No, there's no need, I'm obviously not missing. I said I'm obviously — Look, I just phoned to say, no, I just phoned to say goodbye. *Goodbye*. Got that? okay? No, no need — goodbye —

Frank put the phone down, then picked it up again and called the police. Austen realised that she'd been staring into space and put the receiver down. She imagined the callbox door swinging shut, Melissa coming out of the smell of urine into a clear frost.

Melissa sat in the weak moonlight, curled like an animal. She had scaled the locked gate, swung over the spikes at the top, letting her rucksack thud on to the grass beyond the gravel, and she had landed more or less noiselessly on the other side. Condensation blanked out the windows in the gate-house. Invisible, silent in the dark, the cold, she made her way to the other side of the graveyard and dropped by a random grave. She leaned back against the stone. Below the silhouette of a stone angel she took the books out of her rucksack. Already today she had ripped the pages out of *Tender is the Night* by F. Scott Fitzgerald (Penguin), *Bliss* by Peter Carey (Faber and Faber), *The Novel Today* edited by

Malcolm Bradbury (Fontana), *Madame Bovary* by Gustave Flaubert (Penguin), *Selected Dramas and Lyrics of Ben Jonson* (publisher Walter Scott, 24 Warwick Lane, Paternoster Row, London in 1886, a favourite), *Memoirs of a Dutiful Daughter* by Simone de Beauvoir (Penguin, another favourite, and after an initial moment of nostalgia, nothing but relief), and finally Joyce's *Dubliners* (Penguin). *Dubliners* she had read again, enjoying it immensely, removing each page as she finished it and leaving it where it fell as she walked or sat. She had never enjoyed reading 'The Dead' so much, she realised, as near to tears she tore the last page, the page about the snow, and let it fall.

Here was a place where no one would stare or comment or shout angrily. She took the first book off the pile, *The Sunday Missal and Prayer Book* (Collins). Out came the table of movable feasts, the prefaces, the order of Mass; she didn't need light to know she was tearing out first Sunday in Advent, second Sunday in Advent, third Sunday in Advent, fourth Sunday in Advent, Christmas, Easter, the whole of the year. Thin leaves fell round her, turned in the grass between the gravestones, rustled across the gravel.

The police were worried. The missing woman or someone pretending to be her had emptied her bank account. They called on Austen and Frank and at the insurance company where Melissa worked. They found Melissa's address book under her bed and contacted everybody in it. Austen told them how she had found the flat and what Melissa had said on the phone, and they took away the car and several ripped up books for forensic examination, opened a file on Austen and tapped her phone. They did the same to Frank, who also told them about his phone call, about his call to Austen, about the weird way Melissa had been acting anyway, and what she'd said the night he left.

They opened a file on each of the employees at the company where Melissa was Information Transferer, which meant she spent the day typing the numbers of accounts from letters and applications into a computer so that people could be traced and monitored by number rather than name.

Meanwhile, Melissa disappeared. Sightings of her filtered back to Austen now and then via Frank, via mutual friends, even via people standing chatting in the bookshop where she worked. Sightings took on an almost mythological quality. Austen told Melissa this in the letter she packed in the box of books she sent to a postal collection point near the American border. The postcard Melissa had sent was a colour photograph, a long American car upside down in a crevasse, above on the edge of the crevasse a house and garden, intact. Melissa's spidery handwriting on the back, in ink that looked faded from the sun, said that she was fine, that where she was writing the card she could smell carnations and coffee, just like in Lawrence's *Mornings in Mexico and Etruscan Places* which she was reading, and please to send the books, whichever Austen chose, from the flat. And to send if possible a similar boxload at the same time annually until there was none left. *I'm rereading almost everything now*, she wrote. *I'm rereading Emily Dickinson in the desert here. It's great. Love, M.* Austen passed the card on to the police, packed the books. *I can't help wondering*, she wrote in the letter, *what you'll do when you run out of books*. There was no reply.

A girl leaning against the poultry section in the supermarket reading a book ripped out the page and dropped it where she stood. A shocked elderly lady watched her tearing her book near the freezer compartment; speechless she watched her drop poems in several different aisles, near the bakery, by the household goods, in the check-out queue. The woman, pale with rage, followed the girl picking up the poems she dropped. Outside the automatic doors she stood in the rain and watched the girl leave. Look what the girl's doing! she called to the people going in. Never in all my life have I seen something so wanton, so disgusting, so wilfully destructive. When I was young we knew the value of things. She turned, caught the eye of one of the people coming out of the doors, she waved the fistful of torn poetry. Look, she pleaded; her eyes were desperate.

On an overnight bus to London a man watched, curious, as a young woman sitting across the aisle reading a book removed each page carefully after she read it. Her clothes were dishevelled, her hair looked like it could do with a good wash, she placed each finished page neatly beside her on the empty seat. At the end of the journey the man let the woman get off the bus before him, picked up the pages, took them to his hotel room and read them. He wondered who she was, where she stayed, how he could contact her so he could read the rest.

A woman standing at a bus stop in a large city found a fragment of paper stuck to her heel. It said on one side something about oaths and resurrections, something she couldn't make sense of. But on the other, words were spaced like poems had been at school, and she read:

> *Celestial recurrences,*
> *The day the flowers come*
> *And when the birds go.*

The woman looked up the word *celestial* in her husband's dictionary when she got home. She thought the words she'd spiked her heel through were beautiful and she folded up the piece of paper and hid it in the secret place inside the lining of her make-up drawer. She didn't tell anyone about finding them.

Austen stands in the bookshop and sells books to people, pressing the buttons on the till with the blank knowledge of an automaton as the multicoloured covers of books, hundreds of books each day, shiny exciting new books, flash past her eyes and into little plastic carrier bags. She tucks the money into the correct compartments. Barnes and Byatt are selling well at the moment, and a new biography of the Kennedys, out for Christmas.

The shop she works in is pleasant, airy, tasteful, stays open late. They play classical music by day and jazzier music in the evenings, the public likes it, people tell Austen all the time what a pleasure it is to shop there. There's a Canadian writers' dumpbin of Atwood and Munro on one side of the doors, on the other there's a special display of new hardback fiction about

Eastern Europe, this month's special interest. The shelves are open and well organised, well stocked. From where Austen stands she can see the whole range of the fiction department stretch down one long wall of the store, hundreds and hundreds of books, a mere echo of the hundreds of others before them. Austen knows it's insufficient, it's all not enough, but she doesn't know what to do. When people want poetry she sends them downstairs. In Melissa's now musty-smelling flat the shelves are gradually emptying; sightings of Austen's friend are rare now. Austen scans the shop, looks at her watch, sighs.

All the Margaret Atwood, gone, all the James Joyce, the Virginia Woolf, the Hardy, Lawrence, Forster. All the Carter and Rushdie, the Puig and Marquez, the Klima and Levi and Calvino and Milosz, all the Spark and the Gunn and the MacDiarmid, all the Shakespeare, all the Coleridge and Keats, the Whitman and Ginsberg, the Proust, the Eliot, the Scott, the thick books, the thin books, all the one-volume obscure poets and novelists, all the known names and the lesser or unknown lost or forgotten names flying immeasurable in the air, settling on the ground like seeds or leaves dropped from the trees, rotting into pieces, blown into the smithereens of meaning. Pages flutter across motorways or farmland, pages break apart, dissolve in rivers or seas, snag on hedges in suburban areas, cling round their roots. Fragments litter a trail that blows in every direction, skidding across roads in foreign cities, mulching in the wet doorways of small shops, tossed by the weather across grassland and prairies.

There are poems in gutters and drains, under the rails laid for trains, pages of novels on the pavements, in the supermarkets,

29

stuck to people's feet or the wheels of their bikes or cars; there are poems in the desert. Somewhere where there are no houses, no people, only sky, wind, a wide-open world, a poem about a dormant grass-covered volcano lies held down half-buried in sand, bleaching in the light and heat like the small skull of a bird.

A quick one

When we were first together we made love all the time. All I really remember of the time is that we made love, I remember it in a blur where occasionally details surface so precisely they're like blades, a blur of us on the bed together or me pressing up against you against the radiator or pulling the curtains in the front room at noon and coming back to the couch, you on it opening your shirt, me opening the buttons on your Chelsea Girl jeans. At that time you would unwrap me like a present, delight yourself, take your time guessing what was inside; I'd unpeel you like I'd

31

unpeel a satsuma, like I'd try to take the peel off in one piece, working slowly round the outer edges with my thumb and first finger, working in a circular motion, easing the fruit out of the skin, then my thumb going in splitting and spreading the pieces, and the effort of excitement and self-control as I'd hold back, hold back the biggest segment till last as the taste of you'd burst each time on my tongue. What a time, a time of covering myself with your smell, the time the telephone rang unanswered and we moved to the rhythm of it subconsciously then realised what we were doing and broke apart laughing, the time we reached down to look at my watch and somehow in some violence of love we'd cracked the glass of its face into a mosaic and time had stopped.

That was the crazy time, everybody gets the crazy time. That was when clothes were worn to be taken off, to be thrown across the room, discarded like the friends who stopped speaking to us because you or I didn't turn up to meet them at the cinema when we'd said we would, or because we'd have to reschedule coffee with them knowing we'd rather be with each other, because when they wanted us they couldn't have us because we were having each other. With pleasure, for breakfast, dinner, tea, me with my nose in your hair, you with your hand tangled in my hair, we'd make animal lightness of both the day and the night. We did it all, we'd rub slowly together, we'd fuck hard, we'd lie sweat-stuck on each other, still in each other, waiting for the breath enough to start circling slowly once more, the quick flicker of a tongue, the slip of teeth closing round nipple to sharpen the appetite again. We ate each other up, spat each other voluptuously out, a sticky new creation; several times a day we were God, we made each other. Of course it had to stop somewhere. Of course it did.

I'm trying to remember how long we had of it, the unconditional, uncontextualised sex, and at the same time I'm walking along the pavement avoiding the cracks between the paving stones. We had about two months, I think, of long slow breathing and sheer breathlessness, before we took baths to get clean rather than to experiment or to see what each other looked like beaded and steamy. Eight or so weekends, I make it, before Sunday morning was clogged up with the Sunday papers all over the bed and you caressed me, abstracted, with print-smudged fingers, and we spent the morning reading about Goebbels or Marlene Dietrich. Sixty days or so before I began to smell of paint again and you found the smell and taste too acrid on me and complained about it, even though you'd said you liked it at the beginning, you'd found it – what was it? Exotic or erotic, exotic, I think. Still, sixty days pretty undiluted, not bad. I can think of colder ways to spend a winter.

It's spring but it's cold, so bitter cold that I'm wishing I hadn't lost my gloves. I've spent the morning taking photographs round the city trying to inspire myself and I've left my gloves on a railing or traffic bollard near the statue of Greyfriars Bobby where I took the witty picture of the real dog underneath looking up. I hope someone who needs the gloves has found them, they were leather. The sun's out and the sky's a clear blue but ten minutes ago it was hailing and the pavement's still edged in hail, there are white lines of it on the road where the cars haven't crushed it. There's paint under my nails. I push my hands deeper in my pockets and make myself walk more slowly. In the very beginning you even fished the blue shirt out of the laundry box to wrap it round your face to 'get the smell of art'. Sixty days, it takes less than sixty days for the smell of art to dissipate. I went back up into the loft with the notion that I could paint some of it, the time, and I ended the week hurling great slabs of colour at the wall, then I hurled the chair and the coffee maker and my dinner after them, I threw the coffee maker so hard that the plug yanked itself out of the wall socket, the dinner plate made a dent in the plaster that's still there. After that it was easy enough to get on with work again.

I get to the café at ten past. It's upmarket and dark, and I scrutinise all the people in case I'm simply not recognising you, I have the sudden realisation that I'm not sure I'll know you. I look round the corner but there's no one who might be you there either. You may have been and gone already, it's ten past. You may not even be coming after all. There are two women behind the counter, one about my age, one maybe a bit older; I recognise them from other times I've been in. I get myself a coffee from the younger dapper one, who froths the milk up with a flourish at the machine and flashes me a cool smile. It's trendy here, the seats are carved out of huge lumps of tree. There are framed old photographs all round the walls, of the different cafés the city's had over the century. I scan them to see if I can make out any landmarks, any of the streets, while I scoop the froth off the top of my coffee with my tea-spoon and let it slide on to the saucer. The music playing is country music; booming out of the speaker just above and behind my head is someone not as good as Patsy Cline singing Patsy Cline songs. She's singing about how she's falling to pieces. Each time the voice hits one particular note it hurts my ears.

The woman who served me the coffee is clearing the table next to mine, and she's saying something to me. I tell her I'm sorry and ask what it was she said again. I was miles away, actual years away now, running old footage in my head where you're looking at me and I'm looking at you in broad day-light, and it's just the moment before your arms come up and round and mine drop helpless by my side and your mouth is on mine for the first time ever there on the pavement right in the middle of people passing and staring and people driving with their heads turning in their car windows to look as they pass, and it feels like the street or my body's exploding into little flowers opening their mouths all at once like one of those nature fast-films, clouds hurtle jet-propelled over our heads, things are happening faster than sound, and at the same time these people walking round us with their eyes wide and their mouths agape as I part from you amazed are passing us in slow motion, as if their arms and legs are mov-ing in water instead of air. I look up and say sorry, and ask the woman what it was she said. She's smiling, showing her teeth, they're very level and white. She tells me I was miles away, asks if I'd like a coffee without the froth since I don't seem to like froth, she can make me up a plain one, it's no problem at all if I'd like. I thank her and say it's very kind. She tells me I haven't been in here for ages, have I? She's wearing

one of those little badges that say 'Smile!' and then underneath in smaller writing, 'It makes people wonder what you
were up to last night!' I start reading it and she stops long
enough to let me, and then turns on her heel singing and
swings off between the tables.

The first synthetic chords of the song called 'Crazy' plink-
plunka across the café, and it's then on cue, like in a film, that
you appear in the doorway, pause for an inestimable moment
to let your hair fall back into shape, and in that moment I
remember all the reasons I thought you lovely and all the reasons I didn't like you. We give each other a big hug to say
hello, we are overjoyed to see each other. There's a sheepish
grin on your face, apologetic, sorry you're late, you sit down,
you say how much you love Patsy Cline, she's so brilliant. The
woman brings me the coffee she promised, and asks what
you'd like. You tell her you'd like an espresso and then you tell
her that if she checks it she'll find that the treble is too low and
the bass is too high on their sound system.

We tell each other things for about an hour and during it we
allow ourselves to look at each other coyly from time to time.
You ask me how it was in the States. I tell you I had a really
brilliant time and about the really nice people I met. I ask you
what you're working on. You tell me about the book about the
catacombs of Sicily, how brilliant it was out there though you
preferred the mainland really. You ask me what I'm working
on. I tell you about how I'm supposed to be working on the
commission but that instead I'm in the middle of Two People,
Two Armchairs and a Dog. You ask me to describe it. I tell you
that there are these two people in it sitting in armchairs

watching TV and there's a dog at the feet of one of them. You say you'd have to see it. I tell you I've been taking photos all morning to try to get myself going on The City At The End Of The Century but it doesn't seem to be gelling. You say you're sure it will and look at me coyly. You ask to see my camera. It's just a Kodak Instamatic so that I can carry it in my pocket but you want to see it anyway. I tell you about the dog and the statue and my gloves. Your eyes glaze over. We tell each other some private things. You tell me about your recent break-up with your most recent lover, how messy it was, how violent, how you've only just escaped unscathed. Your face changes colour as you talk about it. I tell you about the last time we ate out together and how I had food poisoning but was too proud to say anything about it. You say so that's where you kept going and we laugh. You tell me about your mountaineering holiday in Nepal where some of the people on it got really sick with fevers and delusions because they drank the water. You tell me a lot about the mountains in Nepal and the people on the trip, and then you look at your watch and say you have to be in London again by the evening. I say I'll walk you to the station.

On the way to the station, in the slant of Princes Street gardens, I take some photos which I'm hoping will help. I take a photo of some office-dressed people laughing and eating Marks and Spencer sandwiches on a bench and a photo of an old woman with a plastic bag round her shoulders delving through a rubbish bin. You say they'll make a good contrast and I say yes, that's the point. I have one photo left to take so against my better judgement I find myself taking one of you, catching you by surprise. You're caught open and smiling against a backdrop of frozen crocuses like a wall behind you, purple and yellow and white. It will look like a casual picture of some ingenue model of the sixties or seventies, or the snapshot on the album cover of some hopeful young girl folksinger. After I've taken it I'm secretly pleased.

We say goodbye and see you again, and you go down into the station. I walk back along the gardens past where I took the photographs. It's colder than in the morning, I'm colder, and I find I've not only left my gloves somewhere stupid but I've lost my scarf, I must have left it at the café. When I get back there and ask the woman who's behind the counter she looks at me knowingly and calls through the back to her friend, the nice one who gave me the free coffee, who comes through saying, oh good you came back then, and rummages about below the counter. She gives me back my scarf, it's been folded smoothly and neatly into a square. I thank her and just as I'm turning to go she makes a noise as if to say something. She looks round to see that her friend isn't listening and leans forward so no one in the café will hear, she says she's glad I left my scarf because it meant I came back and she could say this, she hopes she's not making a mistake or offending me or stepping on anybody else's territory or, you know, but would I like to, how would I like to go for something to eat or a drink or a coffee or something maybe later today or maybe later in the week. I notice there's a red patch on her neck that's flushing right up past her ears. She says oh God she's made such a fool of herself, she didn't mean to put me on the spot, she's so sorry. I tell her no, she hasn't, that I'm really flattered and it's really nice, and that she just took me aback for a minute.

38

She has quite pretty eyes. I write down my phone number for her on one of the paper napkins, tell her to let it ring for a long time because I might be up in the loft, and then I go to get my photographs developed; there are some places where you can get them done in an hour.

Jenny Robertson your friend is not coming

My friend Elizabeth and I were going to the cinema and had arranged to meet at a small Italian restaurant beforehand for something to eat. It's nice there my friend Elizabeth told me on the phone, not too smart and not too expensive and the food's lovely. It was a fine quite warm summer evening and I walked down to the grassmarket and waited for her leaning against the door of the restaurant, except that where I leant against the door, the dust marked my jacket which was a bit of a pain but I didn't say, and I saw Elizabeth come along the street, and we sat down and took our jackets off.

We were in a window seat in the sun, which I always like, but a waiter came up to us almost at once, just after we'd taken our jackets off and settled down actually, and asked us if we'd move to a darker seat because this table was reserved. So we moved, but I wasn't as keen on the darker seat, it was too dark. And the other problem was that it was nearer the back of the restaurant and there was one long table in there, well two or three tables pushed together the way they do, and the people at that table were rather rowdy and had been drinking quite a bit and kept calling at us since we were two girls out. So it was a bit of a calamity that we didn't have the window seat as far as I was concerned, especially since it was only reserved for staff members like the waiter and the woman at the till to have their breaks and coffees at, a thing which rather annoyed me after I realised that's what was afoot.

After our antipasta course and just as we were starting on our lasagne my friend Elizabeth noticed someone she knew come in, and called her over. It was Greta, I hadn't met her before or anything but I'd heard about her from Elizabeth who often mentioned her, they were friends at university. Elizabeth had told me more than once the story of how Greta's mother had called her daughter Greta because when she was giving birth to her, in the final pushes, the doctor told her to count backwards from thirty to nothing, to concentrate on the numbers, and Greta's mother being a film lover immediately remembered the story about the director of a film called *Queen Christina* telling Greta Garbo who was in the film to stare ahead and count backwards from thirty, and that's the final thing you see at the end of the film. It's the most beautiful shot of her there was, the most beautiful thirty seconds of cinema there is and there ever will be, Elizabeth said once to me, there she is, standing on the prow of a great ship, looking towards a future without her lover, her dead lover, the lover she'd decided to give up her kingdom for, and she's staring out to sea, out into the void, and the camera draws nearer and nearer, and for thirty seconds there's the sheer beauty of another human being. And guess what, there she is, counting backwards in her head, thirty twenty-nine twenty-eight twenty-seven, under all that beauty.

Well as far as I could see that would simply take the beauty away knowing that's what she was doing, not that I'm in the habit of finding other women beautiful anyway. Though I haven't seen the film. But that's how Elizabeth talks. I've never met anybody who talks like she does.

This friend Greta came over and sat with us and to be honest I wish she hadn't because the problem with Greta is that she's been ill for a long time and it's very hard to concentrate on anything else never mind just eat your lasagne if there's an ill person in your midst. To give Greta her due she didn't mention it or anything and when Elizabeth asked her how she'd been she didn't go on about it for ages or anything. But even so just having an ill person there. And with those dark circles round the eyes, under her eyes while you're eating. And that thin way the neck gets. I didn't like the lasagne very much anyway because it had been microwaved and I burned my tongue on the first mouthful, and the fork I had wasn't very clean, so really the restaurant turned out to be a bit of a failure.

But then Elizabeth would go and invite Greta to come to the

cinema with us. And so off we went and already I was worrying about how I'd avoid sitting, you know, next. But we had a
nice walk to the cinema in the evening sun, very jovial out for
a night out together. When we arrived at the cinema and were
paying for the tickets Elizabeth noticed a notice, stuck up with
bluetac at the front of the ticket kiosk. It said: Jenny Robertson
your friend will not be coming. Elizabeth read it out loud and
laughed the way she does that means that she's seen something
and thought something clever about it. Greta looked at it and
read it out loud too and said oh, that's so sad, there's something really sad about it. I agreed, yes I said, it's a shame, isn't
it, she'll have come all the way to the cinema and she'll have to
go all the way back home unless she wants to sit through the
film by herself. It would be a bit of a pain if she lives far away,
and what if she's paid for a taxi? Inside my head though I was
thinking that if Jenny Robertson had turned up just at that
moment then probably Elizabeth would have known her from
somewhere and have asked *her* to join us too.

The film was quite good, it was one of Elizabeth's
favourites, that's why we'd gone. It was about these two boys
in school in the war and one of them is Jewish and the other
isn't and the Nazis get the Jewish one and take him away in the
end. It was in French and I understood quite a lot of it though
I haven't been to France like she has. I liked it but I could tell
what was going to happen at the end. But it was a bit unex-
pected in that they didn't have any film of the camps. After the
film when Elizabeth had gone to the bathroom and I was left
with Greta I couldn't think of anything to say so I asked her
about her mother counting backwards when she gave birth.

44

She looked at me blankly, so I explained more fully, about the film director and the counting thirty backwards and the beauty and the doctor and her mother. She was looking at me as if I was mad, and luckily Elizabeth came back just at that moment and I didn't have to carry on the conversation.

We stood outside the cinema by the road and Elizabeth said she'd see Greta home because they lived in the same direction and Greta said thanks Liz, and Elizabeth asked me would I be all right. I said of course I would and it was quite funny because we were the only people at the bus stops and I stood at a bus stop on one side of the road and they stood at the one on the opposite side of the road, and we had a giggle and waved for a while on either side of the road, then their bus came and went and left their bus stop empty. I had to wait for mine twenty minutes in the dark, and when it came I had to put a pound in the machine for my ticket and it was one of those buses that don't give you back your change.

To the cinema

I

There's the cinema, the ticket-tearer, the person whose ticket gets torn in two and the film playing in the dark. Today's film is *Les Enfants du Paradis*, a revived French classic made nearly half a century ago when Hitler was shown in the newsreels with an affable smile on his face, the Eiffel Tower his backdrop. It was made at a time when people in Paris who went to the cinema were forced to watch this image, the doors barred by the armed police who would stand near the screen and watch over the audience to see that any reactions were the correct ones. It is a sumptuous film set in the nineteenth century, about a woman who refuses to be owned by any one of her many admirers, even by the man she truly loves; to her audience when the film was first released she came to stand for a liberated France. After the war the actress who played her was imprisoned for a short while for collaboration; during the shooting she had had an affair with a German officer.

The film is in black and white and it lasts over three hours. It ends on the image of the woman's true lover, after their only night of passion, seeing her disappear. She melts into a street filled with carnival revellers and noise, she is carried away aloft and separate in a waiting carriage. He is left calling her name, caught up in a sea of indifferent people. Today as the curtains close on the end of the film the audience actually applauds, is animated and slow to leave. People marvel at the clarity of the print, they talk excitedly and wave their arms about as they filter through the fire exit into the sun. It's still my favourite film, it's probably my favourite film of all time, one man is heard to say. It's so romantic, I loved every minute of it, says a woman, I thought it would be very long but I didn't even notice the time passing.

Les Enfants du Paradis is a sure bet. Even on a Sunday morning with a ten a.m. start the people who run the cinema know it will bring in a good box-office return. It does so every time they show it; this morning the queue of people waiting for the cinema to open stretched round the corner into the next street.

Or maybe the film this morning is a more recent classic, something like *North by Northwest* or *Barbarella* or *Taxi Driver* or *Betty Blue*. Or a very recent film, already a classic, like *Reservoir*

Dogs. A fading cinemascope musical, an arthouse film, a thriller, as long as it's a classic, that's what gets them up and brings them in on a Sunday. Usually anything black and white or silent or made in France in the fifties or sixties is a classic; films with cult status, very long or very controversial films also count. It's good to have something with a bit of cinematic history; perhaps the film this morning is D.W. Griffith's *The Birth of a Nation*, made in 1915 and described in the programme notes, with references to Steven Spielberg and Spike Lee, as 'the single most important movie in the evolution of the screen'. This is the film that made heroes out of the Ku Klux Klan. Today's audience makes aghast knowing noises when the vitriolic racism of the classic is at its most obvious.

Or maybe it's a French New Wave double bill, a Truffaut and a Rivette. Or no, today at the cinema there's a Screen Goddess double bill, two films starring the silent movie star Louise Brooks, both made in the years just before her immense fame first faded. The first on the bill is the celebrated *Pandora's Box*, the second is the less well known *Beauty Prize*, released in 1930, it's a rare opportunity to see it today. In *Beauty Prize* Brooks is an ordinary young woman leading a humdrum existence until she enters a beauty contest, wins, and goes on to become a famous film star. At the end she is shot dead in a cinema as she watches her own film, killed by her lover, jealous of her success, maddened by his loss of her. She dies below a screen filled with her own giant face, that's the end, the curtains close and the lights come on and the audience leaves in search of Sunday lunch and the papers.

The person who tears the tickets at the door of the cinema

on Sunday mornings is slipping between the empty rows picking up whatever the audience has dropped, to leave the cinema pleasant for the next ticket-tearer and the afternoon's audience. She stops and straightens up, one hand holding crisp bags and discarded programmes; she frowns. She goes to the bin in the entrance hall and pushes this morning's rubbish well down into it.

The cinema is empty, the last of the audience out of the toilets, out of the back seats and gone. The ticket-tearer heaves the fire doors shut from the inside. She doesn't see that outside, leaning against the wall opposite, watching as the doors are closed, someone is there. Someone is standing there still holding the half-torn piece of ticket from today's film stuck with sweat to the palm of one hand. The ticket is the same as all the other Sunday morning tickets, it is grey, it has words printed on both sides. On one side the torn ticket says Admit One; on the other, Available At Time Of Issue Only. A few moments after the doors have closed there is nobody at all in the street outside.

II

I had the postcard of Louise Brooks on my wall in the Klipframe for years before I even knew who she was. Black helmet of hair, black lips, white profile, white string of pearls. Lying dead below the picture of herself. Imagine her arriving at the gates of heaven, I wonder which her it was. If she was older, her bone structure would have been even more

50

remarkable. So much nearer the surface. I wonder if it was the drunken her, the one lying on the filthy chaise longue with the gin bottle stretching the stitches in the pocket of her dress, one moment looking at the ceiling, the next yelling and swearing with that stunning articulacy at God for making life such an unfaithful whore. Or was it the star, the lit beauty, the innocent who knows it all, the girl light enough to swing on the large man's arm as if it's a trapeze in that film this morning, swinging saucily past St Peter in a soft-focus halo like a latter-day saint, smiling shyly at the Virgin Mary, ready to seduce God into giving her a blessed kiss and a starring role?

What a joke. Even if there were such a thing as a good Catholic heaven you wouldn't enter it bodily, only Jesus and Mary were allowed to do that. There's only advertising. There's only adverts, everything on television, the movies. At least here there's a sense of occasion, at least it still feels like there's a dignity, a cheap dignity, about it. I think I love that most, how tacky it is. Somebody somewhere will be watching, somebody will care. That's the promise, and the lie.

The difference is that it feels good when I get up on Sunday mornings now. Almost exactly a year ago I stopped going to Mass. One week there I was, I was saying the words and doing the sitting and kneeling and standing like everybody else, and I noticed a couple, middle-aged I guessed from their back view. Holidaymakers, going by the hopeful clothes. There were crutches leaning between them and at all the kneeling parts of the Mass so far they had stayed sitting. Now it was time for the Consecration and everybody knelt down except these people. When I lifted my head I saw they were standing.

The priest at the altar left too long a pause between one line and the next, the Mass came to a halt. This was the priest who had decided that the main doors at the back of the church would be locked at Communion to stop people leaving straight after it, because leaving before the final blessing, he said, was as impolite to God as leaving halfway through a wedding would be to the bride and groom. The one who had given a sermon a few months ago on how ridiculous and blasphemous it was that women in America wanted to be ordained and in certain liberal places had made priests use 'she' instead of 'he' for God throughout the Mass. Unthinkable that He had a sex, he said. The one who, in one of the first Masses I ever went to in this town, announced without explanation that the most evil and wicked man of the twentieth century wasn't Hitler or Stalin, but Andy Warhol. Priests come and go in your life if you grow up Catholic, and I think I've known priests of all sorts. Some seemed truly holy men, some fools, some very learned, some could make you feel that something real was happening in the Mass without you having to try as hard as with others. Now the man who had stopped and looked up from his book at the altar, the man staring at the standing couple among the kneeling people, made something real happen for me.

People whose heads had been bowed looked up now to see why there was a sudden silence in the wrong place. The priest, the only other person standing, leaned forward and spoke into his microphone. At this point in the Mass, he said, we, the gathered congregation of this Church, do not *stand*. We, the gathered congregation of this Church, *kneel*. Those who do not wish to adhere to the sanctified ritual of this Mass in this holy place should not expect to celebrate the Mass here.

I could see the back of the neck of the standing man, it had gone a bright red. His wife was flustering with the crutches. I watched the man struggle to get to some kind of stiff kneeling position, I watched his wife, already down, giving him her arm. I heard the priest's nasal monotone start again over our heads and then I stood up. The people kneeling in my row had to sit up to let me past. I turned and walked down the aisle to the back, I put my hymnsheet on the spare pile and I crossed to where the big glass doors were. The doors were automatic like doors at airports and railway stations, they had been installed the year before and hailed as an important modernisation for the church. They weren't yet locked for Communion, they slid open as soon as I stepped on the rubber and I heard them hiss smoothly shut behind me a few seconds later sealing in the Mass. I went to the newsagent's and bought the papers as usual, and I went home and made Geoff and myself a huge and greasy breakfast, bad for our hearts, which we ate in bed. That was the last time I went. I didn't even go at Christmas. Now I let people in here instead, I watch the film with them from the special folding chair – even if the cinema's packed I still have an excellent view, one of the best in the place. As soon as the end credits begin I run across in the dark to the fire exit doors and throw them open. The daylight blazes in when you do that, the people sitting in the seats nearest the doors turn their heads to shy away from it. My senses are good in the dark now, they have to be. Part of the job is making sure

nobody illicitly smokes or talks or does anything that might dis-
turb anyone else, like eating things out of scrunchy paper or
plastic. Then, after everyone else has gone, I pick up the rubbish left between the rows, the applecores and empty cans, the
dropped half-tickets. The occasional condom.

The projector here makes a noise like faraway heavy rain.
Sometimes it's a shock to open the doors and see that the pavement's dry and the sky's clear. I savour even the moments
before I let the people in to sit down. The decayed paint on the
walls. The carpet trodden into paths. The curtains over the
screen humming across by themselves like some Victorian
magic trick.

I hadn't realised it made Geoff so angry that I like it so
much. Chris and Mike came to supper last night and I saw it
for what it was, we were sitting at deadlock over the tuna
salad. It especially seems to anger him that I pick up other
people's litter, the cinema should have a machine for that,
apparently, or it should be done by a cleaner or teenagers with
no GCSEs. I was stopped in my tracks when he said this. I was
left holding my fork, a slick piece of egg on it an inch from my
mouth. I'd been declaiming Belmondo and Seberg at them, *tu
es vraiment dégueulasse*. I'd been trying to explain the way the
film jumps about on purpose, so that in the same second the
people on screen might still be in the same place but because
there's been a tiny jump-edit they've moved on, they're in a
different place altogether too. Chris said she'd started watching *A Bout de Souffle* on TV and had got bored with it, had
switched it off. Nothing's as good on TV, what could I say? I'd
been telling them how people had walked out of the Woody

Allen film because the hand-held camera had made them feel
sick. Like a fool I'd even been singing them bits of the song the
girl sings at the beginning of *Beauty and the Beast*, trying to
explain how it is that a cartoon scene can be as good as, better
than, one in a real-life film. God, I was saying, anything's possible. I was probably talking too much. I was certainly being far
too enthusiastic for good taste.

It's as well I stopped when I did. I'd been just about to tell
them how ridiculously pleased with myself I am if someone's
dropped money between the seats and I find it. The week
before last I picked up three pounds fifty off the floor. Twenty
thousand a year and I'm excited when I find an illicit three
pounds fifty. I could hear it jingling in my pocket when I left
the cinema, I bought a ham sandwich and the Sunday papers
with it and ate the sandwich reading in the sun, sitting on the
wall outside the shopping centre. That's when I read in the
papers what we'd been shown all week on television, that in
Bosnia there were people cutting off other people's heads with
chainsaws, and about the camps where women are kept especially for rape. I sat there for a long time but I didn't know
what to do about it, or even how to make myself believe it. I
looked at the pictures very hard. I didn't get home until four
and my arms had gone brown from the sun. I told Geoff it had
been a very long film, it was my first lie for quite a while and
it left me full of adrenalin.

Geoff made up cappuccinos, he shouted across the noise of
the machine that it was my vulgar streak that made me want to
work at the cinema, and we all laughed, he and Mike especially. It's interesting that he reacts like that. I don't know what

else to call it. Before, years ago when we first started, one night when we were new at our curling into each other in the dark, he told me what had made him decide he loved me. He had been off work with flu, watching afternoon television, flicking channels aimlessly, and he aimlessly began watching a terrible film on Channel Four where a man dressed in sixties clothing is cycling round some green and pretty parts of London on a bike too small for him. He goes freewheeling down a hill when suddenly he realises the brakes on his bike don't work, and he ends up smashing into a massive billboard advertising Raleigh Bikes. When he opens his eyes at the foot of the billboard the first thing he sees is the model advertising the bicycles, and he falls in love with her. That's what it was like, he whispered to me. It was like smashing into a billboard with your name written all over it, your picture ten feet high. I couldn't help myself, he said. I stroked his head. I knew what he meant. I was happy. I was happy for quite a long time really.

But now it's all so obvious. We've done all the right things, we've got the jobs, we've bought the flat, we've eaten out at all the restaurants, we've paid for the groceries in cash and the luxuries on our access cards, we've even started talking about doing the evening classes in Italian and Art. Worse, Chris is pregnant, she told us last night. Mike was very excited. Geoff got excited. It's what I hate most about it, the predictability. Eventually I tried to change the subject. I didn't dare talk about films any more, the only other thing I could think to tell them about was the letter I read in the paper from the priest who was writing a book about the phenomenon of rosaries that spontaneously change colour. He wanted to know when, where and under what circumstances people's rosaries changed, and whether there was any particular pattern to the change. It didn't really work. That's what shagging's all about after all, Geoff said to me after, while I was washing up. His arms snaked round me from behind and his tongue blocked my ear. God. I hate that word, shagging. Geoff got very angry before he fell asleep, afterwards his breathing kept me awake for hours, I eventually got some sleep on the couch. His breathing has been keeping me awake for weeks.

I'd work here all day every day if I could, I wish my whole week was spent like this, with music to tell you when and what to feel, and I could sleep through the films I'd already seen. I'd give up my salary in a minute; all I do is spend it on things I don't really want. Friday was standard enough, the Christmas catalogue copy. I had to do the mailshot and colour supplement leaflet, aimed mainly at busy housewives and older people who don't have the energy to go to the shops. Christmas is a magical time, and we all look forward to Christmas preparations with the special excitement of children. But wouldn't it be bliss if you could do all that dreaded Christmas shopping this year without even leaving the comfort of your armchair? With Homeshop your Christmas wish can come true. Whether it's an unusual or fun-packed item for a friend, or that something special for someone very important, we've got all your Christmas shopping under wraps. No stamp needed! The Christmas Homeshop Catalogue is our gift to you.

Be confidential, be informal, be warm, use the word *special* as much as possible. It was my idea to send everyone who fills in the reply-paid coupon a free small stuffed polar bear holding a Christmas tree, to do a run with a no strings gift as the main theme, Huggles the Bear Will Help You Shop From Home With Homeshop. They were very pleased with it as a concept, it brings families to the centre of the promotion, kids will demand the free bear, mothers will read the catalogue. A gift to their children. All's right with the world. I'd done well again. I'm a high flyer.

I watch the pre-film adverts here; this girl in a white volkswagen draws up to the edge of a cliff. It's dark, she's crying, her elbow shows bare through her shirt with a faint sensuality, a faint sense of breast. She looks devastated, tired, sad, it's all over. Suddenly she notices her Nescafé in the back of the car, she plugs a heating element into her dashboard, and with some mineral water she also just happens to have she makes herself a cup of it. It's dawn, she drinks it, the sun's out, she feels better. It's going to be a bright bright bright sunshiny day. No matter how dark it seems, no matter how much you've cried, with instant coffee there'll always be another day.

It's true after all. If you believe it, it's true. I hate it. I love it. I love this place, it tells people lies all week, and on Sunday mornings it tells them classics. When I go home after working here my pockets are full of the stubs of their tickets. On a wet Sunday it fills up fast with people, with the smell of wet animal. On a hot Sunday the air conditioning blurs into action, we're glad of the dark, the big cool cave. Whatever the weather we take the commercials willingly, like sweetened vitamin pills, then we sit back and let the films go right inside us. The next few Sunday mornings will be good. On the other side of *The Seventh Seal* there's a Marx Brothers film, there's *Rashomon* and then there's a restored print of *The Wizard of Oz*, Judy Garland shining in that too-tight gingham pinafore, in the ruby slippers, skipping round the spiral of the yellow brick road again. Kansas she says is the name of the star, that's what the Good Witch sings. I know so much of it by heart. Lions and tigers and bears – oh my! That's what Dorothy, the Scarecrow and the Tin Man say when they're scared going into the dark wood. They link arms and chant it over and over again. Lions and tigers and bears – oh my. It'll be good to see it.

III

I am in love with the girl who tears the tickets at the door of the cinema on Sunday mornings. I love her. I love her desperately. I have never been so desperately in love.

I can't eat. I don't sleep. My mouth is dry and my tongue sticks to the roof of it. I think about her all the time. When I give her my ticket to tear sometimes our hands touch. Her fingers are beautiful, she bites her nails, I've seen her. Her knuckles are beautiful. When I pass her on the steps every week and she gives me my piece of ticket back and sometimes she smiles at me, I can't get myself to breathe properly, it's like something is stuck in the back of my throat. When I sit down in the cinema and I think of how there's just thin air between us it feels as if something in my body is strung so tight it will snap and I'll fall in pieces on the ground. She doesn't even notice.

She never notices me watching. I watch her in the dark all the time and she doesn't even know.

In the light from the film playing I can see her profile. I can see every time she changes her sitting position. I can see her putting her fingers in her mouth. Rubbing her eye. Running her hand through her hair. Rubbing her nose, pushing at the muscles in her neck. She makes little creaking noises shifting in the chair as she crosses or uncrosses her legs, or folds her arms, or leans forward with her elbows resting on her thighs. I love the sounds that she makes. I listen for her to cough or clear her throat or sniff. Sometimes she falls asleep in the middle of a film. I see the moment she shuts her eyes and the moment she opens them again. I watch everything about her. Once she took her shoes off, she pushed them off with her feet, I couldn't see properly without leaning too far over the person sitting next to me. But once I was the only person in the cinema with her before the film started, for almost five minutes. Five whole minutes, just me and her. As the lights went down the rows of empty chairs between us were like waiting cats.

I have saved all my torn tickets since she started putting them in my hand. I keep them in the suitcase under the bed. Every Sunday I add another one. I lie on the bed in the dark. If we were on a bus trip together and she were to fall out of the emergency door down the side of a dangerous cliff, I would jump down after her as fast as anything and save her from falling into the ravine by catching her hand just at the moment when she couldn't hold on to the tree root any longer, I would climb up the side of the cliff with her on my back, her arms round my neck, and everybody on the bus would clap as we reached the top and she opened her eyes. If we were standing over a fiery pit with flames leaping at us, and I was given the choice of which of us would be flung into it, me or her, I wouldn't hesitate, I would throw myself into the furnace and disappear down amongst the molten rocks never to return. She would realise then how much I would give for her. If we were lost in the desert, she and I, and we had had no water for two days, and all we had was a peach, I would sit on the burning sand and take the peach and peel the velvet off with my teeth for her, I would give her the peeled peach, put the flesh of it wet into her hand, maybe hold it to her mouth for her, if she'd let me, so that her lips wouldn't be cracked. Then she would know, then she would give herself over to me. Then I can take out the her that I keep in my head, then I can pull all the strings, make her do what I want and what I like. In the morning my tongue is stuck to the roof of my mouth again.

Except on Sunday morning, Sunday morning is different. I like to drop things on the floor, I know she'll be the one picking them up. One time I wrapped up chewing gum in a piece of silver paper and left it, so I could have the thought of her picking it up still warm from my mouth inside the paper. I drop money sometimes. I like to think she could be in a shop buying something with money that came out of my hand. I am careful not to drop too much because then she might give it in at the box office and not spend it herself.

We are getting very close now. I have been allowing myself to sit one seat closer each week. Now that it's summer she wears open-topped shirts and I'm close enough to see her collarbone. The hollow of it is one of the places I think about touching. I don't know what I will do when I reach the chair closest to her. Perhaps before that we'll meet in a shop or at the supermarket and she will look at me and realise, and say, oh, you come to the cinema, don't you, why don't we go for a cup of coffee? Or I'll say, oh, I see you when I come to the cinema, don't I, and she'll say, yes, I feel like I know you very well because I see you every week, and I'll say, let's go for a cup of coffee and she'll say, yes, like that. I'll ask her if she'd like to come out for a drink with me, or if she'd like to go to the cinema, and she'll laugh. Then we'll be friends, that'll be the start. I'm always watching out for her when I'm at the supermarket or in town at the shops. But I've never seen her anywhere else. I only ever see her when I go to the cinema. It is the only place I can find her, she's there every week. I go every week. I have loved her since the very first moment I saw her there.

IV

It's Sunday morning again. The cinema is three-quarters full, the lights go down. The ticket-tearer shuts the outer doors, pulls the curtain across, shuts one of the inner doors and waits there with one door still open for latecomers. The screen curtains draw back. A picture is behind them, Greek pillars with the words Pearl and Dean suspended in a blue sky, there is a fanfare of trumpets. Then there are pictures of a tropical beach, a parrot, a beautiful thin dark woman with long legs and inviting eyes, and then some people drinking Bacardi in a bar next to the ocean, which they speed across by motorboat under a perfect night sky. Next, a young man walks through an American town followed by many people and buries his jeans in a hole in the ground. A young woman drives her car to the edge of a cliff and makes herself a cup of coffee. An escaped prisoner breaks back into his cell bringing cornflakes for his cellmates. A man walks across a desert and bangs his head on a giant beer bottle.

And now the main feature. A woman melts into a street filled with carnival revellers and noise leaving her lover calling her name in a sea of people. A man runs across a field, he is being chased by an aeroplane. A woman is caught in a machine which gives her orgasms. A man shaves almost all his hair off and covers his body in hidden guns. A man suffocates his girl-friend in a hospital because she has gone blind and mad. Some men shoot each other in a warehouse. A woman wanders through a hospital silently playing the banjo to wounded soldiers. A boy runs away from a reform school to the sea. Two women enter a house full of ghosts to rescue a little girl. A woman is stabbed by Jack the Ripper at Christmas-time. A woman is shot in a cinema by her lover. A man is shot by policemen while his lover who betrayed him looks on pretending she doesn't understand his last words to her. A middle-aged man tells the camera why he doesn't love his wife any more. A young girl bored with her provincial life falls in love with a beast. A man on a bicycle, the brakes of which don't work, hits a billboard and knocks himself out. Death plays chess. An orchestra floats out to sea. Some people sitting in the pouring rain listen to several versions of the same murder story. A girl and her dog are trapped in a house thrown high into the sky by a tornado, she opens the door in black and white and finds herself in technicolor paradise. It is only the beginning, all sorts of things will happen. It's well worth the price of a ticket.

The touching of wood

Today we're standing in the ruins of a village taking pictures of the houses because they're falling apart. Straggly olive trees and other kinds we don't know the names of are growing through the places where so many floors have been. Some of the houses still have roofs, some just have sky. Geraniums are growing wild, bright red; down in the light and the dust at the end of the shadowed pathway the combination of sun and the colour of the flowers is a shock, beautiful, hard on the eyes.

We are four days into our holiday with three days left. We have one Kodak Gold spool left each; in a rush of fever I

bought six for a bargain price at the duty free shop at the air-
port and we've been feveredly taking photographs since.
Hundreds of other tourists have come here today too; each
time another tour boat docks at the shore another fifty or sixty
stagger down the walkway to take photos of each other wandering through the remains of the crumbling houses. We're
more artistic and more thoughtful than that, of course; we're
both going out of our way to get photos with no people at all
in them, to preserve the strange sense of abandonment the
place has.

Stone and wood on water and rock. Thirty years ago people were still living in these houses, well, dying in them. I
take a picture of a window-frame with some broken glass
still stuck in it, and look around me. The village is a mixture
of rubble and greenery, I'm not sure whether what's left of it
is holding out against or being forced apart by the plants and
flowers and trees. There are doors and door-frames warping
in the stone; some of the shutters look like they'd easily work
even after thirty years. I don't dare touch in case, what if it
fell apart in my hand, though there are no signs up to say we
shouldn't. Visitors to the island can do pretty much what
they want; they can go inside most of the shells of the houses
and trace the rooms if they like, though a few of the doorways have planks nailed across them to keep people out,
unsafe.

We have one hour before we have to be back at the boat; the
man who gave us the talk about the island made sure we all had
tickets before we got off so we can get back on again. Mine is
number 58, yours is 57. I check on you secretly to see if you're

feeling all right. You're so much better it's frightening. Four days in a hot place and the black lines round your eyes have almost gone, you're who you used to be, you're full of energy and intelligence again, funny and fast, all coloured in by the sun. The best thing is I don't wake up in the middle of the night and find you've gone, here you manage to sleep right through, we wake up facing each other. Last night I was sitting reading on the balcony and you came and leaned right over, you looked carefully below and to the right and the left, you said, I'm just checking that we're not going to traumatise any little children or ordinary families from Newcastle, and you leaned against the shutter and put your arms round my neck and with your tongue you pushed an olive into my mouth, it was warm, I ate it.

That was a good game, we played it until late. I have the stone from the first kiss in my pocket now, hard, grained and grooved, I turn it over in my fingers. I watch you as you get into position to take a picture of one of the doors we're not allowed to go through. You wind your camera on and wait for the sudden surge of German people to clear before you take it. Behind the door, which is hanging off its hinges, we can see rocks and sea; the water round this place is bluer and clearer than anywhere I've ever been, turquoise at the rocks below, then purple, shelving away to a deep light blue between here and the mainland, which isn't very far off. I don't know what else to do other than lean over a wall and take a picture, try to get all the colours in. Apparently the people who were left here used to give the authorities a real headache by escaping to the mainland all the time, that's what the boat captain told us.

Before we got here the boat anchored in a place called the Blue Lagoon so people could have a swim if they wanted, but where we anchored the lagoon was full of small jellyfish, we watched them over the rails, hundreds of them hanging breathing in the water. So the boat moved to another cove, also called the Blue Lagoon. The people in charge of the tour split us into groups of German, Dutch and English speakers, and our guide, the captain, explained to us about the island we were going to visit.

He had fished there as a boy, he told us, he had made friends with the lepers from the safe distance of his dinghy, and eventually he had become the only person who didn't have the disease to set foot on the island while the lepers were still there. Set foot, he said, that was a good but a sad phrase, because now he could tell us that so many of the lepers he knew had lost their feet, and their toes. And it was a sad fact that lepers had been shipped to this place from all over Greece, even after the cure for leprosy had been found.

The captain's name was Manolis. I am a fisherman still, he said. In the day I take you here with Buzz Travel, my Travel Organisation which is the biggest on the east coast, in the night I fish. He told us about the four different types of leprosy, about how people who had it would carry it without knowing for seven years and then it would explode inside them. In some people for instance their eyes would frost and crack like a glass, in some there would be a loss of feeling in their bodies like an anaesthetic that never goes away. The bodies would just get smaller and smaller, he had photographs and press cuttings in a special book in the cabin if any one of us would like to see it, he had been collecting this since the colony was finished in 1957, he used to show them to groups but had eight years ago stopped because of upsetting the children if there were any.

He passed round a tattered photograph stuck on cardboard, a picture of two women; one of them had an arrow, inked in red, pointing to her hand. The one without fingers is the lady I knew from the island, he said, look at the hand, the one without fingers is the lady. Because when I last saw her she was only this size, she had only a torso and a head, it is very sad. He passed round another, a picture of Aristotle Onassis and a woman, and told the story of how Onassis and his sister tried to buy the island, how he wanted to flatten the village and turn it into a casino, it is lucky he didn't, he said, he could have turned our beautiful island into an inferno with yachts and traffic like the south of France. He told us about how a clever Greek prince had at last worked out the way to get rid of the Turks who'd had control of the fort on the island for so long, and the way to do it was to land a rowing-boat full of lepers on the island – yes, it worked, the Turks were, fzzzz, gone in a few hours, haha. And that's ladies and gentlemen how it all started. And although we think it's finished, it is not. There are still thousands of thousands of people with leprosy the world over, yes even now, and curiously the only other species in the world to be able to have leprosy is the armadillo. But now I will sail you to the island, I wish you to enjoy the island, and remember to tell your friends about the special tour of Buzz Travel, he said, and the boat swung out of the Blue Lagoon with Greek music playing over the loudspeaker, and we arrived at the island, and walked down the walkway to take our photographs.

You've scrambled right up the side of one of the houses so you can take a picture of some writing carved in the stone above the door. I look at you up there, you are handsome and preoccupied, it strikes me again that you're beginning to look older, like a woman, not a girl any more. But you hang over the front of the doorway like a girl, holding on to the branch of one of the trees so you can get right up close. You call down to me. What language is it, is it Greek or Turkish? I wonder what it says? you say.

The thing is, it's so beautiful here, we weren't prepared for that. The flowers everywhere, the birds, the colours of the sea. You jump down, land on your feet by me and pick up one of the branches that snapped off when you jumped.

You're always picking up bits of wood, you always have, ever since we started; the window-sills at home are lined with the twigs you snap off trees or the shards of wood you find at your feet. Stones are dead, you said to me once when we were at the coast, you liked the touch of wood. Stones were just bits of bigger dead stone. Wood was alive like stones never were, life went through it, that was what wood was. I told you you were being precious again and you got indignant, I had to do a lot of teasing about your precious wood collection before I could get you to smile and come out of the mood.

You break a piece off it and tuck it into the back pocket of your shorts, and you squint up and pretend to read the writing, you say: Lost Property Office. Ear and Nose Department.

Lost an Ear? Find it Here. Limbs, Fingers and Toes Enquire Two Doors Down.

I tell you you're sick. Yes, you say, but they can't keep me here, they can't, they can't, I'll swim to the shore, I'll make for the mainland. You can't swim, I say. I'll build a raft, you say, I'll use this door, this one, here. I'll tie these trees together, I'll make a lifejacket out of branches and leaves. I'll get there, never fear. They'll never catch me.

The island takes half an hour to walk round; we walk past the fortress, the hospital, the graveyard for the rich and the charnel houses for the poor, the sea shimmers to our left and all the way round we torture each other with terrible jokes. We look through a slithole in the fortress wall, you say it's probably a leperbox. I say something about how a leper can't change its spots. You dance along the pathway between the other tourists singing under your breath so that only I can hear, the words *I sent a leper to my love and on the way I dropped it*. People look at us. We pretend we don't see them. We jostle each other, knock against each other, like teenagers laughing and feeling guilty at the same time.

Back on the boat you fall asleep, and miss seeing the dolphins and the pirates' cave and the island where the sacred goats are kept, they're jumping about on the cliffs but it's too far away to take a picture. I tell you about them while we wait for the bus. You fall asleep on the bus too. I shake you on the shoulder a little, careful not to touch the sunburn, when we're back in the fishing village where our self-catering is.

We ignore all the signs offering English Breakfast and Pizza and Fish and Chips, and we go to the café where there's no

71

menu, the one on the harbour front with the octopuses hanging stretched out to dry above the outside tables. The girl recognises us, she's friendly, smiling, she comes to sit at our table to take our order. But she can hardly speak any English and we know hardly any Greek. We try to explain that we want what we had before, we want aubergine and courgette, but she looks confused. She points to the octopus. We say no. She takes us inside and shows us trays of fresh white fish and chicken, she shows us vine leaves on a plate in the fridge and skewered chunks of pork sprinkled with herbs, but we're shaking our heads and laughing, standing helplessly, you're shrugging your shoulders, I'm waving my hands about, we can't think how to say it. She remembers the English for colour, what colour? she asks. You remember the Greek for delicious. She laughs and laughs, she holds her side laughing, she calls through to the cook who laughs too, she exclaims, what colour is it, delicious, and holds on to the counter laughing. Other people at the tables outside are looking in, trying to see what the fuss is about.

We have chicken and stuffed vine leaves instead, and a lot of very sweet wine, I drink most of it and the day settles into a red flushed sunset behind you. We take photographs of each other sitting opposite. You take seven of me in as many seconds, most of them will have my arms up over my face. You swing back in your chair and work it out, you say, we'll have two hundred and sixteen pictures, a hundred and eight each. And two Saturdays from now we'll be at home, probably looking at the pictures and saying, that's where we were two Saturdays ago.

We talk about where we'll go tomorrow. We could go and visit the Church of Arcady where all the people were killed, but that would take a substantial bite out of what money we have left. Or, if you haven't overdone it today, we could hire bikes and cycle round the side of the mountains to the next town, though it looks like it may be no different from the one we're in now, a few ramshackle houses, a lot of apartment buildings, a rash of new grey concrete waiting to be apartment buildings, several supermarkets and everywhere else places for English and German visitors to eat. We can't decide, it's a nice feeling not having to. Now it's dark and so we leave a big tip, wave goodbye to the girl and stroll, slowly because you're tired, up to one of the supermarkets for chocolate. Easter is late here, tonight it's the night before Palm Sunday, and as we pass the little church the sound of men singing the service is mixed with the old Dexy's Midnight Runners hit from the nightclub across the road, we sing along, *but not us, no not us, we are far too young and clever*.

Back at the apartment you go for a shower and I smoke on the balcony, sitting in the noise of crickets, holding my cigarette so as to keep the mosquitoes out of the room. The fridge hums. Water comes slowly to the boil on one of the rings and I hear you singing. Inside there's the smell of salt and suntan oil, out here of something perfumed, some night scented plant. The moon is huge, much bigger than at home.

I shut the shutters and come in to make some tea. The room is plain with white walls, most of it is taken up by the bed, a mattress sunk in a kind of stone mould, with the only decoration in the room the dark carved wood-panelling on the wall at its head. The bed is still unmade, clean and crumpled from the night before. I clear the table to make space for the cups; it's covered with the junk we've accumulated in just four days, the bus tickets, the leaflets and tickets for museums and ancient sites, the guide books and the film spools in plastic containers with our initials inked on the tops, the white stones and the bits of wood we've picked up on the stony beaches, the flight tickets. I'm not looking forward to the flight back. On the way here it was me, after all, who was most scared when the plane took a turbulence dive, shuddering seven miles up in the sky; when we landed at dawn on the rubbly runway I saw there were patches of sweat on my thighs where my hands had been. I decide not to think about it. I make the tea and I make the bed, I fold the fur blanket down ready for tonight.

It's later tonight I have the terrifying dream, the one I will only remember having in two Saturdays' time when we're looking at the photos. I dream that I am looking at you in a beautiful landscape, and the more I look at you the more my eyes freeze over, and I know that each time I look, because you are so beautiful, scratches are forming over my eyes like someone scratching on a negative and soon I'll never see you or this beautiful place again. I try to tell you but you're getting smaller and smaller and further and further away, bits are splintering off you as you move, you're laughing and waving but eventually you're so small I don't know where you've gone.

I wake up in a fever and I don't know why, I can't see anything because it's so dark with the shutters, and I can't remember why my heart is beating so fast. Then I hear you breathing and I know we're on holiday and you're next to me,

I hear a change in your breathing because you sense I'm awake. I feel you turn towards me. Before I let myself fold inside you, before I push my head into your arms and my eyes against your shoulder, I do what I realise you've been doing all along, I reach out above our heads and for luck, for love, for a moment I'm touching wood.

Cold iron

What can I tell you? The sea and the snow and the wind.

Earth and then grass and then snow settling on the grass. Snow choking the narrow gravel paths, nestling into the neck and filling the stone eyes of a praying angel, silently mittening the leafless branches of trees, muffling the spruces. Over the iron railings, outside the great gate the sounds of a city bound and gagged by a few inches of snow, the soft blur of car wheels and engines. Above the city and above the grey snow clouds, more dark night sky; go up further into black space, the darkness broken only by the lumps of rock that (our stars, our futures) promise us light, wonder, constancy. Not visible tonight from below. Beneath, back on the ground and into the earth – through it, cold, hard – below snow grass soil packed tight the dead are lying quiet in their boxes holding their breath, waiting to be opened, like disappointed presents.

Snow falls, nothing happens.

I'm telling you. My mother died while the closing credits of 'EastEnders' rolled on the portable colour television my father had put up in the corner of the room where they'd set up the special bed with the special cushions. That's what my brother told me on the phone, I mean about the credits, so that made it a couple of minutes before eight, he said. I was six hundred miles away and I had been out of the house for the first time that day to get something to eat, going to the shops in the dark. The phone must have rung in an empty house. When I opened the door it was ringing, and there was the distance. We hadn't known when, but then it was, and there was nothing to do but sit, nothing to do but hang on till the morning and get the train along the coastline through the snow.

The first dream I ever had was full of snow. Perhaps it wasn't my first, there were surely others, babies dream all the time. But this I think is the first one I remembered when I woke up. I was very young, two years old, and in the dream I'm standing outside our front garden and outside our front gate, I'm wearing my new red coat, my mother had bought it for me because we were going to Ireland to see her mother. That's real, that's not just the dream. We didn't go in the end;

a couple of days before we were due to leave her mother died so I never met her. What I can remember is not really knowing what Ireland meant, or what Granny meant, wondering in my head were they interchangeable words.

In the dream I'm dressed in red standing outside our front gate in deep snow, and I look up at all the houses on our street, along both sides. All along the street people are leaning out of the upstairs windows of the houses, looking down at me and smiling, waving. They're paper people, paper cutouts, they flap their thin arms when they wave, they're all coloured in with crayons, very bright colours, yellows and blues. They've got thick black lines that mark their clothes and their outlines, and the colours go over the lines like they do when you can't yet get the crayons to stay inside the lines. Their faces are black lines too but not coloured in, still paper-white, and they're smiling. And then this thing happens. A great wind blows, I hear it behind me and it blows past me. It gathers all the people up out of the windows and the people blow away into the sky. I watch them disappearing over the rooftops.

What I was telling you. My brother is older than I am, he works at the BBC so things like how many minutes to eight 'EastEnders' finishes have some meaning for him. I had been home visiting two days before at the weekend, and had helped her to get up and go through to the bathroom, had watched, stunned yet not in the least surprised, as my mother struggled out of the circle of two of us holding her up and somehow made her way through into the kitchen demanding that we light her a cigarette, her bones almost visible through her skin.

So I travelled back down on the Monday, and when I got there the phone rang and my sister told me things were worse, suddenly, but that still we didn't know when, still she was remarkably strong, through of course the drugs. And to hang on, no point in coming all the way back up. So I phoned next morning at half past eight and my father, harried, the phone had been ringing constantly and he'd been having trouble forcing my mother to swallow the several types of painkiller, passed the phone to her, a portable phone, one of those that crackle so you can't hear anything if they're held a certain way, and my mother spoke to me but I couldn't hear. So I went back to bed, and slept, and tried to work in the afternoon until someone phoned about the coma.

I walk around the streets and it feels like I'm always walking against a tide, all sorts of rubbish floating on it, my head full of stuff, packed like a junk shop. When I sleep I'm wakened by the murmuring of something round my head, worrying at me like fruitflies round a windfall.

My mother's ear, dainty and perfect in profile as she eats at the dinner-table, cutting up food pensively with her fork.

Once we watched a programme about Irving Berlin and how he put two basic formulae together to make one song, once she even stayed up and watched a late night film with me, it was good, I think it was *Metropolis*.

The day I was waiting for a lift to the station to go back down south and she was ironing and talked about the war, the men who went up and didn't come back from the air, saying cheery goodbyes to people in the canteen and knowing you might never see them again. That's when she told me the story of when she was on a weekend's leave *staying with your aunty, but I was due to go back on at 4.30 and had to get the bus down in the morning, so I was ironing my skirt, we had this horrible sergeant who would slap you on report without so much as look at you if your buttons weren't sparkling or your shoes. So I was getting ready to go, I was ironing my uniform, I was singing away, my head in the clouds, or looking at the sky out of the window or something stupid, and the next time I looked down there was this great burn in the skirt, I'd burnt it! And I only had a couple of hours before the bus, and I didn't know what to do. So I pulled on my coat and I ran as fast as I could, I used to be able to run quite fast you know, to the tailor's on Queensgate, and the man looked at the skirt, and he looked at me like this, oh no he said, I don't think I can do anything with this, look at the state of it. And I said please could he try, and that I had to get the bus at lunchtime, so he said to me go home and have a cup of tea and come back and I'll see what I can do. And when I went back, there was my skirt, and you couldn't see that there had ever been a burn, you couldn't even see where he'd done any mending. And the tailor wouldn't take any money, he wouldn't take any money from me.*

Warne's Observer's Picture Cards. 32 Cards in Full Colour with Descriptive Text. I: British Birds II: Wild Flowers. Every set consists of 32 cards, each of which bears on one side a picture in full colour of an individual breed or species and on the back a panel of clear descriptive text explaining the distinguishing features of the subject. Frederick Warne & Co., Limited, London and New York. I found them in the bureau under the birth certificates and old official letters, and took them away with me without telling anyone, complete sets, yellowing a little. I don't remember ever having seen them before. Tiny browned holes, drawing-pin marks, at the top of some of them. Blackbird, swallow, chaffinch, house martin, house sparrow, mistle thrush, hedge sparrow, robin. Primrose, red poppy, wood anemone, cowslip, buttercup, forget-me-not, bluebell.

Post Office, Inverness, Telephone Inverness 600 Extension 1, 13 January 1949. Dear Miss Ann MacGregor, In connection with your recent interview regarding employment as a Temporary Telephonist, I have to inform you that you successfully passed the suitability test. I regret however, that in view of your engagement to be married in the near future, it would not be in the interests of the Department to incur the expense of training an operator whose services may be available for a limited period only. It is with reluctance, therefore, that I am unable to offer you the position. Yours faithfully, William C Forsyth, Head Postmaster.

I was fourteen, I was walking along the road at the back of the canal going to the fair illicitly with Caroline and Christine, and we had been talking and laughing about boys, then somehow we were serious with that carefulness about real things, asking Caroline what she could remember of her mother. I don't really remember much, she said, but I do remember her coming into my bedroom one night to show me her dress before she went out to a dance. It was really beautiful, I remember that, it was really beautiful, it was white.

The little toy dog is covered with dust, Something something something, The little tin soldier is covered with rust. Two little orphans a boy and a girl, Sat by an old church door. An Irish boy was leaving, Leaving his native home. Laughing

82

under her breath at me crying at them, all towelled up after my bath.

I've come to the conclusion. There was driftwood along the beach I went to last week, but it was oily. There were shells whose ridges were stained with dirt from the sea, where the waves were black, that's not what you expect of waves. But I put the shells in my pocket anyway and only tossed away the dirtier ones, throwing them back into the sea, tricking the seagulls though not on purpose that it was food I was throwing. I walked out along a stone sort of pier, like a broad wall sticking right out into the sea with a railing running the length of it for people to hold on to against the wind, the sea on either side. On the left side the water lapped on the stones leaving a line of wet leaves, on the other the water was that filthy colour I was talking about; where the white bubbles usually form from the waves' movement, on this sea the spume was grey.

I didn't just find shells. I found a piece of that pottery that's blue and white, and the thing about it was that it had been shaped into a smooth triangle by the sea, and that on it in blue were printed circular and triangular shapes, the pattern was almost as if it was meant to just be that small triangle though it wasn't, it was a broken piece of something, it had been smoothed into its shape by sheer chance. I found a piece of glass too, made round, green and made smooth, like a bit of one of those old thick-glass bottles. The good thing was that these weren't blackened by the oil or whatever.

Because things don't make the shape we expect them to. Because there's never the conclusion we imagine, not really. After I hung up the phone I sat down to wait for whatever it was and my head filled suddenly with green and the vision of a girl I'd never seen before, smiling, laughing actually, and the place was in the sun, and this laughing girl took me as far into it as I could go, but that wasn't very far, it wasn't a place for me to know. She had as casually as you unzip, untie, undo the last buttons of the shapes you leave behind, stepped out, and as casually as a forties filmstar that people all know and love but can't remember the name of, waved goodbye, said it was all all right, the war would end soon. And that's where the credits rolled, and the screen went blank (the end of the reel) then white as the lights came back on.

It's then you're left on the outside, a mere member of the audience, one of millions, and the thing you saw, the thing you were part of has gone, it was just the play of light and movement through tiny frozen images.

That's when the murmuring starts eating at you. That's when you're at sea.

I put the shells in a bowl on top of the television when I got home from the coast, and put the piece of pottery on the mantelpiece, and I gave the bit of glass to a friend who put it on her bookshelf. Her way of doing it is different from mine. She says her father disappeared one day, went to sea in a sieve and, not surprisingly, it sank, but that the villagers put it down to the fact that he must have met a woman (possibly a witch) on the way to the harbour, or he must have got his feet wet before he got on to the boat. Or a witch must have rowed out to sink him in an eggshell someone hadn't smashed through the bottom of with a teaspoon. Or maybe, she says, he'd been foolish enough to speak out loud the forbidden words on board, the words that summon the devil, words like pig or salmon or rabbit, then forgotten to touch cold iron to lift the curse.

That's what she thought. Myself I'm hanging on, leaning on the rail that overlooks the sea on either side of me, I'm picking up bits and pieces for my house. I'm thinking it out, I'm working out the story.

College

Two men in T-shirts got out of the van and one opened its back door and climbed in. They unloaded the bench, shifting the weight to and from each other, first to get it out of the van and then as a kind of game, calling to each other when one caught the other out. They carried it under the archway and into the gardens. Led by Dr Crane they swung it along the gravel paths between the lawns, with the Bursar, the parents and the dead girl's sister following behind. Then Dr Crane strode out across the grass and stood with her arms outstretched, and the men put the bench down. One of them spoke for a moment with the Bursar, who signed a piece of paper, and the men left. The parents, the girl and the two College officials stood round facing the bench.

The wood of the bench was of a very light brown and had a strong sweet smell. On the top back slat were carved the words and numbers

IN MEMORY OF GILLIAN YOUNG 1972–1992

The five people stood in front of it. Birds sang into their silence. After a moment Dr Crane cleared her throat and suggested to the mother that she might read out the Principal's letter, and the mother got the letter out of her shoulder bag again and read it out, including the College address and all the bits about the Principal being called urgently away to France. She sent her very best to Mr and Mrs Young whom she had met at the memorial service. She had of course been only too sorry at the tragic circumstances of that first meeting. She thought the gesture of the bench a very fine one. Your daughter's friends will sit on it on summer days and think of her, as will women at this college for years after her own year has been long gone from our care, the Principal's letter said.

Then Dr Crane took one step backwards. Well, she said, I suggest you let me take you now for a little sherry in the SCR, to take us out of this heat and let you relax before lunch. I'm sure we can find some fruit juice or a lemonade for your, for young Alex.

This gave the Bursar, who had a blinding headache, the chance to excuse himself and get back to his office and the problems of the rest of the afternoon, 2.00: the meeting about the graduate heating bill; 3.15: the drafting of the conference press advertisement; 4.00: the caterers.

Stupid woman didn't even realise she'd made a joke. Crane. Like that bird with the long legs. If she was one of those birds her legs would snap. Never survive, genetically top-heavy. *Young Alex. If Young Alex would like a lemonade.*

She knew this was unfair and that the woman had actually been quite nice. But knowing that made her feel worse. Crane, more like some great McAlpine sticking her great arm out like who did she think she was. Like Margaret Thatcher or Queen Elizabeth the First or someone, Put The Bench Here My Man. And that creepy bald man and the creepy way he looked at you. Brook, like the poncey awful poet you had to do in second year in the war module, think only this of me forever England if I should die.

This was a very different England from home, like a foreign country really. Even the weather felt like abroad or like it wasn't real. Like a pretend place put up for a film, all the buildings constructed so people could film a story about history or really rich people, the Royals or *Pride and Prejudice*. When she'd said that as they drove past the colleges her father had said it *was* a foreign country, either that or a different planet, and her mother had got angry and said it was a beautiful place and that Gillian had loved it here. A silence had filled the car. They'd only been in the same place with each other for ten minutes and already it was hopeless. Alex had sat in the car and told herself five times over, don't say anything, don't say anything at all. Once, after Gillian, and after her father had gone the first time, she'd opened her eyes in the middle of the night, the bed wet with sweat and her blood going round so fast that that's what had woken her, it's my fault, it's my fault pounding in her head. It had taken all that night in the dark to build the wall between her and the thought, and the wall came out made of sullenness. In the back of the car driving through the town Gill had lived in, Alex had looked carefully out of the window making sure she didn't say anything else.

Now she was trying to sit very still on the bed. The room the woman had found for her was in what was called the Sick Bay, it said that on a wooden notice screwed on to the outside swing door. It was narrow and white, and there was a smell of gas in it and a notice sellotaped to the grill of the gas fire, Do Not Use. In one corner of the room was a cupboard full of wooden crutches, in another there was a folded wheelchair. She tried not to look at the wheelchair. It was so old-looking it might have dated from the first world war. You could have used it in a film about the war, it would have looked authentic. This whole place could be in it, one of those grand houses for war-wounded poets to get better in. The bed was like a hospital bed, very high off the ground with white-painted iron bars at the head and the foot of it. You had to sort of jump backwards to get up on to it and when you did it made that creaky noise, and was too soft, so that already even before you'd slept on it your back felt sore.

She got down off the bed as carefully as possible and went to open the window. It was stiff, but after a bit of forcing she could put her head and shoulders out. The air was warmer outside the room than in it. From here she could see the length of the College, its weird colour orangey-red against the green of its lawns. The tall windows painted white against the red gave it an outraged look, like a lot of shocked wide open eyes, she thought, or like something baring its teeth. That was called anthropomorphism, to think that, to pretend that something had a personality or was like a person when it wasn't really. For instance that wheelchair couldn't really be evil or horrible, it was just an object even if it looked horrible. In English it was called personification. Alex was quite good at school and had got even better at it since her parents had split up.

From here you could see the bench. She watched it as it sat in the space of the lawn. It looked small and the wrong colour; the other benches and tables in the gardens were a much darker brown, almost black compared to it, like they'd been soaked in black water. She saw two men carrying stepladders past the bench, and could see another man mowing the grass far out on the pitch beyond the gardens. His mower made a faint buzzing noise. The gardens were noisy with birdsong and there were still some students wandering with books and tennis racquets under their arms; she heard them calling across the early evening in accents she found high-pitched and irritating.

The men had put the stepladders up in the archway and seemed to be poking about at the nests. She wished she'd never pointed them out to the woman, she always always spoke before thinking and now look. They were being seen to, like the man said. The precious rafters. The Crane had explained at lunch about how they were fixed together, holding the roof of the arch up on their own tension alone, so they'd never needed

91

to be bolted. So if they were so strong, what difference would a couple of birds' nests make? she'd asked. Her mother had given her a look, and a row after lunch in the toilets about insolence, her father had told her she didn't know anything about architecture. People were stupid, they were so stupid. Like the bridge they'd passed on their walk and her mother had said someone, not Darwin but someone, had put it together on its own tension and then later someone else had taken it apart to see how it had been made and then not been able to put it back together again so it had to be nailed after all. People were stupid, you'd think they'd know. You'd think they'd know not to do things, know not to do something like go scuba diving when they had earache from a cold. You'd think they'd be told, or that someone would check before they'd be allowed to do it. People always had to do things, take things apart or go and look at things that were nothing to do with them. If people had been supposed to look at the bottom of the sea then the sea wouldn't be there. Or something.

The mower droned in the distance and the smell of cut grass drifted across. Alex realised that the birdsong was growing louder, birds calling to each other across the grounds in a mess of noise. The harmonies they made sounded like they were by mistake. She watched to see if she could see them. How do they die? she wondered to herself, and what happens to the ones who live all the way to the end, who manage to avoid the cats and the cars and the kestrels, and the falling out of nests before they can fly or the humans poking at their nests when they're still in eggs? Or being pecked to death by other birds, or flying into plate glass they can't see and think is sky. What happens, do they shut their eyes – do birds have eyelids, even? – or tuck their beaks under their wings one night then just not wake up for the next dawn chorus? Do they get colds, do they drown? Do they feel ill like people do, do they stow themselves away like dogs and cats in some quiet place and wait? She could see a blackbird listening for worms on the lawn below. How does a blackbird die, does it die in mid-air in a seizure, its heart stopping with a twinge and a rush of fear like if an aeroplane engine were suddenly to cut out in the middle of the sky and the air give way below its wings and the ground come up to meet it? Do they stop being able to breathe, do they panic, do they know?

As she leaned looking out of the window two girls arm in arm, one in white, one in pink, neither of them looked anything like Gill, walked across the grass to where the bench was and stopped next to it. One was talking, the other leaning on the arm of it nodding and listening. Then she saw the girl speaking stop and point, and the girl on the edge of the bench turned too, read the words and jumped off the arm as if it were hot. They stood back, both reading its words. Then they went away.

She felt funny when she saw that, like she had that afternoon when she had gone searching round the College for the room number that used to come home on the tops of the letters and the backs of their envelopes. A plain white wooden door with a handle, 204 in plain black painted numerals on the door. 204 Old Hall she had written to, 204 Old Hall Gill had written back. This was Old Hall, this was 204, this was the place she had gone to, this was one of the places she hadn't come

93

back from. As Alex stood there the door next to this one had opened with a rattle and a girl with long black hair had come out carrying a saucepan full of baked beans, had pulled her door closed behind her and had padded across to a room opposite where there was a cooker. She had been wearing slippers and humming a tune that was playing in the room, and the funny feeling had come.

She leaned hard against the window-sill to crush the place it felt funny in her stomach, she thought about how good it would feel to push her stomach against hard wood until it hurt so much that you wouldn't notice the funny feeling anyway. She watched the girls walk away from the bench. She took the stairs at a run so fast that she nearly fell down them. Along the corridor, out across the flagstones and the gravel, across the weak grass with the sign saying Please Keep Off This Grass. There was the bench and as the sun's last shadows stretched across the garden to fill its words and dates the dead girl's sister sat down square in the middle of it.

She sat forward with her legs apart and her feet on the grass. Then she sat with her back pressing into its back, then she spread her arms out along the top of it. Wheeling high above her head – were they swifts? were they swallows? swifts by the sound and the tails, arrowheads screeching against the sky. She sat there for a long time, the air around her grew damp, began to be chilly. The dark came and she pulled her feet up on to the bench, hugging her knees to her chest.

Another garden, another big house, the sun out again, too hot. Another bench, no name on it or date but it had a fancy back, it wasn't just any old bench like you'd find in a park, because the dead people who had lived here had been rich and famous. You'd have to be rich to live here, it was like a castle, or at least what was left of one.

An elderly woman was sitting beside Alex; she was wearing a badge that said National Trust and the name of the place on it. She was just what those girls from the College would grow into, big-toothed, full-blown, annoying her here, thinking she had the right just to talk to anyone who happened to be sitting on the same bench as her. She was talking about the roses growing in a wandering bush next to the seat and although Alex was nodding politely, she was willing the woman to leave her alone, and it felt like something inside her head was too big for her face and skull.

These roses, the woman was saying now, friendly, educational, these roses are old roses. By that my dear I mean they're the original form of the rose. What you now think is a rose and call a rose wasn't the first. The first roses were these, like this, and she held a rose on the bush up in her hand for Alex to see. The famous garden shimmered in a heat haze; there was no wind. Are you a member of the National Trust? asked the woman. Alex shook her head and made an effort at a smile. Well, the woman went on, it's an excellent thing for a girl your age, ask your parents about it.

Alex scanned the gardens from where she sat, but she couldn't see them. She had seen an expanse of purple flowers against a wall, she had seen a place where the flowers were all supposed to be white, though a notice was hung in it to tell visitors that the flowers would be at their best some months later. She had seen statues in all corners of the gardens, the statues of girls placed among the flowers, one with its head bowed and no arms, the stone of it a yellowed white against a hedge; one made of black metal, standing with its finger poised at its mouth like it was supposed to be thinking, its hair carved back off its face, its eyes blank sockets and a crack forming in the metal of its forehead. And these flowers, all these flowers everywhere, their heads and stems coming up out of the ground. Everywhere the never ending birdsong, people everywhere in these gardens and her mother and father somewhere, she didn't know where.

The note on her mother's College room door that morning had meant they had slept together again, the whole thing was going round again. *Alex, I'm at the Garden House, come for breakfast, get a taxi if you need to, I'll pay, love Mum xxx* and a sketch of how to get there on foot. Here we go, thought Alex holding the note outside the locked door, here we go again.

They should make up their minds, she told herself in her head, like she'd told her friend Janice at school in the far corner of the playing-field the last time it happened. It's like they're big kids, they should just make up their minds and stop playing about. Sometimes he comes round really late and they shout and there's this massive argument and a lot of slamming, then either he storms out or he's there in the morning and it's all nice again for a couple of days. Sometimes I get up and she's gone to his and left me a note saying to make sure I eat breakfast. But you'd think they were old enough to decide what they're doing by now.

When she said it like that it made it a kind of joke, that was a good thing to do and Janice pretty much knew what she was talking about because her parents had divorced when she was small. And it was easy, like she'd said to Janice, to know why they were like that, because of all the things that had happened and everything.

But it didn't make it any easier when you went into the breakfast room and could see them over by the window laughing in that embarrassing way with each other like they were really happy, like they were teenagers locking hands over their greasy plates, even kissing, all the people in the place looking at them, and knowing the whole thing was going round again.

Alex came up to the table without her parents noticing until she was almost upon them. We were wondering when you'd get here, said her mother, pushing her hair back from her face. Get a chair from that table over there. What would you like for breakfast?

The table they were at was only really big enough for two and her father's too-large legs took up most of the room under it. Alex sat down to the side, nonchalant, not caring. They were stupid.

I don't really want anything, she said.

Have a cooked breakfast like we did, said her father. Alex made a face. Her mother started piling plates over to make room. You'd better eat something Alex, she said.

I'm not hungry, said Alex.

How about some toast, said her father, toast and jam?

I don't want anything, Alex said, looking at the ground.

Well, said her father, if she doesn't want anything she doesn't want anything.

Alex, just stop being so adolescent, said her mother. She'll have a breakfast same as we did, get the waitress and order it for her.

No, said Alex. I don't want a cooked breakfast, I'll be sick. I'll have some toast, it's all right.

Or a croissant? Avec du beurre et de confiture de, du — what's the word for strawberries? said her father. He was in a good mood. Come on Alex, what's the word?

Fraises, said Alex almost under her breath.

You'll need something in your stomach for the car, said her mother.

Alex turned to her. I thought we were going home on the train. Is Dad giving us a lift home? She turned to her father.

We're going on a day out, said her father.

There's a place I've always wanted to see again, her mother said. It's in Kent, it's only a couple of hours, three at the most, and your father says he'll drive us there for the day. She looked at Alex's father but spoke to Alex. It's really lovely there, she said. I haven't been there since I was about your age, a bit older maybe, closer to your sister's. I loved it.

I'll give you both a lift back home tomorrow, to the door, said her father. Better than the train any day.

I've got an exam on Monday, said Alex. A waitress put a basket of croissants down on the table and her father took one out and put it on a plate in front of her.

It's not an exam, it's just a class test Alex, said her mother.

But I wanted to revise for it, she said.

Well, we'll be home tomorrow, you can revise tomorrow night, said her father. He was getting edgy. It'll be fun, he said. It's a beautiful garden and anyway your mother wants to see it.

Alex looked at the croissant, thick and dull on her plate. Will you let me listen to my tapes in the car? she asked.

Not your walkman, said her mother.

As many tapes as you want for as long as you want. Within reason, said her father.

Alex broke the croissant with her fingers. Her mother passed the butter but she shook her head no, she only wanted jam, she spread some on. She took a piece on her tongue and pressed it to the roof of her mouth till the jam ran over the sides of her tongue and underneath it. It was too sweet. She was hungry, but this wasn't what she wanted.

And another thing, the old woman was going as she patted her forehead with a handkerchief from her handbag, and another thing, it's only because the lady who lived here cultivated these particular old roses that they came back into fashion, it's only because she went out of her way to nurture them that other gardeners began to take an interest in them again and saw how marvellous they are. They are marvellous, aren't they? It's her cultivating of these beautiful old roses that should have made her famous, not her books at all. She rediscovered a piece of tradition hundreds of years old and almost lost to us, you know. Now we know what roses were like when Shakespeare was alive, because of her. They were like this one.

It was hot, it was so hot. Alex broke out into a sweat. Because what right had this old woman beside her to be this old? What right had she to think this stuff was important? After the woman had got unsteadily up off the bench and said goodbye, and she had said goodbye to her and tried not to show the things in her head, Alex took one of the roses in her hand. The thorns on these old roses were small. The woman was out of sight now and nobody could see her. She wrenched the petals out of the flower on the stem, all in one fist. Then she did the same to another, making sure no one was watching while she did.

She dismembered all the flowers she could reach without drawing attention to herself, and sat back. Petals covered her feet. In her hand, stuck on one of her rings, was one going black already where it had creased. The smell of it was very nice and it felt to her as she smoothed the tips of her fingers over it like the inside of a dog's ear. The smell of these roses was better when they were pulled apart, she thought, than it had been when they were just growing there on the bush.

She found her parents with their heads bent towards each other in the herb garden; her father put his arm round her and her mother gave her a kiss on the cheek. It'll be all right, her mother whispered in her ear. Do you know where we're going now? her father said. We're going on an adventure now, we're going to find a pub with a lunch in it. They walked back to the car park together with Alex in the middle.

It didn't take long to find a pub; it had a sign outside saying Draught Bitter, English Cheeses, Home-Cooked Foods. Perfect, said her father. Inside the room was cool even though it was busy and they sat round a table next to a wall; on the wall a plastic shelf with a perspex front had been fixed into the wood, and the shelf was full of leaflets about things to do and see in the area.

Go on Alex, you decide what we're going to do for the rest of the day, said her father pointing to the leaflets. Her mother smiled at her and reached round the back of her neck to fix her collar for her. Alex pulled out some of the leaflets, one about Kent being the garden of England, one about the place they'd just been to, one about a nearby castle and one about a village a few miles away. When the leaflet about the village was unfolded there was a map of the local area on it, places marked for trout fishing, for Pitch and Putt, a vineyard, some oasthouses and a forest. The village itself was shown on the map by a kind of sign-post, a long pole with a person at the top of it – no, two people – no, it was one figure made out of two people stuck together at the top of it, above them the name of the village.

The food arrived. Alex turned the leaflet round; on its front was some writing and another picture of the figure made of two people. The figure burned itself into her head.

Eliza and Mary Chulkhurst – the Biddenden Maids: Eliza and Mary Chulkhurst were born joined at the hips and shoulders in 1100 and lived 34 years before the first died. Her sister refused to be separated saying 'we came together, we will go together' and died soon after. They bequeathed the Bread and Cheese lands to provide for the village poor and needy. To this day their charity is remembered on Easter Monday at the Old Workhouse. Visitors also may purchase a memorial biscuit bearing an effigy of the Maids.

Is that a good place to go then Alex? asked her father.

No, said Alex. She folded the leaflet up. It looks awful, she said. She put the leaflet under her leg where she sat. It looks like a really boring place, she said. I don't want to go there.

What about this castle then? Her father, his mouth full of bread, picked up another piece of paper.

Are you all right Alex? asked her mother. You look pale.

I think I've just had a bit too much sun, said Alex.

You didn't have enough to eat this morning, said her mother. Try your lunch. It looks nice. Mine's very nice.

Yes, okay, said Alex. I'll be okay in a minute.

All the more for me if you don't want it, said her father doing his old joke of creeping his hand across the table towards her plate. Alex pushed the plate to his hand and stood up. I'll be back in a minute, she said.

She locked the door of the toilet but she wasn't going to be able to stay there long, there were only two for the whole pub. She sat on the seat with the lid down and closed her eyes. Into her head her sister had come, laughing at her. It was evening, an early summer evening, the window open and the birds loud outside and she was lying on her sister's bed – a rare thing this, to be allowed into her sister's room and not chased out, no fight, no yelling or hair-pulling. Her sister was towel-drying her hair at the mirror to go out. What do I do, Alex was saying, her face pressed into a pillow, what do I do if he wants to? I don't know how, what do I have to do?

Alex, you'll know when you do it what to do, you'll just know, Gill was saying, watching her in the mirror. She was lying on the bed picking bits out of the candlewick, her eyes screwed up with the embarrassment of asking, even of the thought. Then Gill was behind her, wet hair cold on her neck, and had rolled her over on to her back laughing in a way that was kind, saying, look, I'll show you, come here, and kissed her full and hard on the mouth.

See, Gill was saying, it's not as difficult as all that, is it? It's nothing to be afraid of, you're *good* at it Alex. Gill shook water from her wet hair over her, pinned her down and laughed at her, they were both laughing hard, and then Alex heard people outside waiting to get into the cubicle so she got up and flushed the water and drew back the bolt.

Gill had been burnt into little pieces of ash and blown away. The front door of the pub was ahead of her and she walked straight out, letting it fall quietly shut behind her, walking through the car park and up the narrow road. She walked for a long time until she came to a main road, then she walked on the grass verge until she came to a petrol station with a shop, where she went inside and bought a litre carton of orange juice. She sat in the shade on a pile of stone slabs next to the shop and drank half of it in one go.

She had stopped crying by now and was waiting for a chance to blow her nose on her shirt, but the petrol station was always busy. Across at the pumps was a small lorry; the man who had been filling it hung the pump back up and came across to the shop. Hello there, he said to her as he walked past her. The same man called something when he came out of the shop but the traffic on the road drowned out what he was saying. He came over to where she was sitting and stood above her.

I said, are you stuck here? Are you waiting for a lift to any-where? the man asked. He had a beard and longish scruffy hair and was wearing a leather waistcoat over his chest. The waistcoat was covered in pouches that looked full of things. He told her he was going as far as Brighton and Hove with a load of frozen foods then back up to the city. Alex thought about it for a moment. She wasn't supposed to do something like this.

I'd like to go and visit my auntie, she said. She lives in Brighton.

I'll give you a lift then if you want, said the man. Quicker than you walking. Haven't you any bags?

I'm not going to visit for very long, just to say hello really, said Alex.

A flying visit, said the man. He opened the passenger door for her. The woman serving behind the shop counter watched through her window as the girl climbed up and the man helped her, she watched the man push the big door shut and get in the other side and she craned her neck to watch the lorry pull out of the petrol station.

The cabin of the lorry was decorated with flags and stickers and the smell of sweat and smoke hung in the air; there were cassettes everywhere, piled on the dashboard, even stuck down the sides of the seat which was so high that Alex's feet swung an inch above the rubbish on the floor. Once they were on the road the man reached up and took something down from behind the sun shield. Look at this, he said to Alex, and gave it to her. It was his passport; inside was his photo, he looked younger in it, and his name and date of birth.

No, look further in, go on, he said. Alex flicked through it. The passport's pages were crammed with the stamps of foreign places.

There's a lot, she said.

I've been all over the place, said the man. All over the place. This is the job for travelling. I was in Germany a couple of days ago. Last week Germany, this week Brighton, next week the north of France. I know all the cities of the world. Well, of Europe.

He pushed a cassette into the machine on the dashboard and the cabin filled with music. I love Rod Stewart, he shouted. When I was your age I had all his records. How old are you?

Sixteen, Alex shouted, and tried to make her face look older. The man didn't even look round.

You probably don't know who Rod Stewart is.

I do, I've heard of him, she said.

So whereabouts does your auntie live in Brighton? the man asked.

Alex didn't know anything about Brighton except that it was near the sea. Near the sea, she yelled.

Runs one of those hotels, does she? said the man.

Yes, said Alex, too loud in the gap left by the end of one song before another.

What's the name of it? The Metro? The Esplanade?

Alex said it wasn't either of those, she couldn't remember the name of it but she'd know it when she saw it. The man asked her if she liked Brighton. She said she quite liked it.

How about if I drop you off in the centre of town? said the man. Alex said that would be great, her auntie lived near the centre of town. The man turned the music up even higher and sang along out of tune. At the songs he particularly liked he got carried away and drove faster, rapping his hands against the steering-wheel and the dashboard almost in time to the music. Alex sat well back in the deep seat and looked out of the window. She realised she was sitting on the side where the driver usually was. This must be a continental lorry. You could see over all the traffic, you could see for miles.

Since you've been gone it's hard to carry on, sang the man and passed Alex some chocolate from one of the pouches. You don't smoke, do you? he asked her. She shook her head. Wise, very wise, he said. Stunts your growth and you're too small as it is. Never start. He lit a cigarette and sent the smoke away from her out of the window at his left arm.

In the busy built-up centre of a town the man stopped the lorry in the queue at a traffic light and reached across Alex to open the door. It swung out into the middle of the road. The sea's down there, he said. Do you know where you're going? Alex said she did. Here, said the man, and fumbled about in one of the pouches. He gave Alex the rest of the chocolate and three twenty pence pieces.

Phone someone and tell them where you are, he said.

All right, said Alex. She jumped down the steep drops from the cabin to the step and the step to the road and the man pulled the door shut. The lights changed; the lorry roared and she braced herself against the draught of its passing. She stood in the middle of the road, trapped by fast traffic on either side of her. Above her the sky was split in two, half light, half black, and she couldn't hear any birds.

Deckchairs piled flat one on top of the other on the pier had a notice next to them saying they were free, but they were all chained together and padlocked. Alex thought that was quite funny. There was a booth where a computer could tell you about yourself from your handwriting; there was a painted gypsy caravan beside it with a sign on its door saying TO LET.

Alex looked at the sea. She could see it below her through the wooden slats she was walking on, thick and green, slapping at the legs of the pier. There were painted sideshows with empty holes cut for faces so people could stick their heads in them and have their photographs taken. The faces of Charles and Di, of Victoria and Albert, if you looked from a certain angle, were filled with sea.

Welcome to the Pleasuredome, said the sign with the huge clown painted above it. Its bow tie rotated and one of its eyelids went endlessly up and down. The Pleasuredome was full of video games. Alex took her purse out. She had about twenty-five pounds; ten pounds from her mother, ten pounds from her father, five pounds she'd taken from the box where she kept money in her room and some loose change from buying the orange juice. And sixty pence from the man in the lorry. At the change cubicle she changed one of the notes into a heavy handful of coins. She tried a trivia machine; she lost several times guessing which horse would come first; she put a pound in a machine and pressed a button and watched the fruits spin. Then she climbed up on to a seat shaped like a motorbike with handlebars and a screen in front of it, and raced at hundreds of miles an hour dying twice, crashing into another bike and swerving too far off the edge of the track. She came ninety-second and would have had the chance to put her initials on to the initials list on the screen but she couldn't work out how to do it before the time limit passed. She was down to her last two pound coins when she found the cowboy video machine.

A large screen was fixed in front of a saddle-shaped seat; stuck on to the right-hand side of the saddle was a holster with a gun in it. Alex took the gun out and a voice told her to try her sharpshootin' luck pardner and save the town. With the gun in her hand she read the instructions. The idea was to sit on the saddle, which would move like a horse, and shoot at the figures who would appear before you in the film on the screen, film of real people. If you shot them before they shot you, you survived. The machine would give you three free practice shots, after that you had to kill villains at the ranch, the bank, the saloon and the corral. Alex put her money in the slot and on her second game she hit all three practice bottles. The sound of ricocheting bullets and glass smashing came out of a speaker at the top of the screen and when you hit the people you could hear them groan and fall.

The real problem was that you tended to hit the inno-cents. People came at you so fast that it was hard to tell who you should and shouldn't shoot; she had killed the lady in crinolines and the kindly old-timer by mistake with her first few bullets. But the more you played the better you got, and she changed her second note into ten coins and pushed them one after the other into the machine. When this money was gone she almost ran to the glum woman in the change cubi-cle. She could have two more games on the cowboy machine and there would still be enough left for something to eat afterwards.

Two older boys were playing on her machine when she got back so she had to wait. But they weren't very good, they were too slow on the draw and their game was over quickly, both of them got by the man in the black hat outside the bank. When they came away from the game she took their place before anybody else could. In the last half hour she had perfected her aim, she had taught herself when and who to kill in each location, and this time she ran up a score so high that the machine awarded her extra time and extra bandits in the corral and the old-timer she had killed in her first game congratulated her from the screen.

The boys had been watching; when she realised this she was glad she hadn't known. Now one of them came up behind her. That was brilliant, he said.

That was quite good, his friend said and spat on the ground. Where'd you learn to shoot like that?

I'll give you a game if you like, the first said, just so you can prove to us it wasn't a fluke. His hair fell over his forehead and he was smiling.

Well, said Alex, okay then.

She won easily. The boy avoided getting shot but ran out of bullets at the second location. He took his defeat graciously. You didn't get extra time this time, I must have put you off, he said. Go on, Dave, you play her too, she's better than me.

No way, said the other, I'd have a snowball's chance.

The boy asked Alex if she'd like to play against him on the Grand Prix machine to give him the chance to win. Alex said no, she hadn't any more money and she had to go now anyway.

Well, see you around then, said the boy as she went, and the other nodded at her. Careful out there, called the first, you'll get soaked, it's going to piss it down.

Alex left the Pleasuredome. She had outwitted a machine and impressed some older boys; people had come at her from all sides with guns and she had been quick and ready. She broke into a fast run along the pier and ran all the way to the end nearest the land, then stopped and leaned over the side. She wasn't even out of breath, but her heart was beating fast. Something was happening. A storm was coming up off the sea, a wad of darkness overhead like the sky was wearing a black hood; the pier and the town had turned grey. Her heart was thumping so hard that she was shaken by it. There was a strange wind, one that seemed to be pushing behind her and against her at the same time. Then she felt two drops of rain, they were cool where they glanced off her arm.

Already there were people clumped in the doorways of the hotels opposite, little groups of people watching the sky from under the booths on the pier. Then there was lightning across the sea, a fraction of light, and the thunder was followed by a wall of rain hitting the ground so hard that a layer of it hovered inches above the pavement.

She went down in the rain on to the beach. There was nobody there but her and rain ran down the back of her neck and along her spine, it slid down her hair and down the sides of her nose, battering her legs and shoulders, streaming off the ends of her fingers. From where she stood through the dark of the rain she could see the pier. The underside was shadowy, the thin supports looked like they would snap at any minute and the whole structure would fall into the sea. She could just make out the small huddled people on top of it, lined up along the sides of its buildings, pushing against each other to be out of the rain. On the beach you could feel the weight of it and the full hammer of the thunder, you were closer for a moment to light that could split the black sky, it was exciting, it was even beautiful to be in the middle of this.

YOU BASTARD she shouted at the sea. YOU BASTARD. She heaved this out of herself with all her force. Then it struck her that the words didn't matter. The sea roared at her. She threw her head back and roared at the sea:

YOAAAAAARH YOOUUUIIIAAAAARH

Her whole body bent and strained with the noise she was making; when the noise had gone all her muscles hurt. It was funny to do this, to be howling at the sea. She was amazed how funny it was and she laughed out loud, but that hurt too. Rain filled her eyes, it ran down her face into her mouth.

She took as deep a breath as she could, filling herself until it was painful. Then she breathed it out, slowly, holding it back then letting it go. She breathed like this, small and drenched at the edge of the sea. She measured its distance with her eyes. She followed the line from the blank horizon all the way back to her own feet on the stones.

She was learning, she told herself. That's what she was doing, she was learning.

Scary

Earlier that evening Tom and I were waiting for our connection. We sat in the café at the station buying coffee
after coffee so we wouldn't feel we had to go out into
the cold and wait on the platform.

Tom and I had really only been together for about a month
but I liked him. He was unusually tender in bed and I liked the
way he kissed, it felt solid and firm. Now I was getting to
meet a long-term girlfriend of his, Zoë, and her partner,
Richard; we were to go through and have supper with them in
their flat in Greenwich, stay the night and come back on the

early train in the morning. It was going to be great for me to meet Zoë, Zoë was wonderful, I'd love her. She'd love me. Tom was looking forward to meeting Richard whom he'd heard so much about. I was feeling nauseous as we sat in the café. Our train was very late, Tom tapped his spoon on the side of his empty cup. He still had his work clothes on, he looked very good in them.

It was dark outside already and very cold. We were sitting near the door of the café so Tom could watch for the train and every time the door opened a blast of cold air hit my back. A man wearing no jacket came in; he stopped at our table and said he had lost all his money when his jacket had been stolen and he needed to get to London. Would we lend him the money, or some of it? he asked. He told the same story at each table round the room. Outside an empty train drew up on the platform and Tom buttoned up his overcoat. I got ready too. The train now standing on Platform 4, said the announcer, terminates here, all change. The doors of the train slid open. Nobody got off or on. The doors slid shut again and the train slid away. Tom looked at his watch.

The man with no jacket was sitting speaking to himself at one of the tables at the back of the café; by the sound of his voice he was getting angrier and angrier. A rail official in a blue suit came out of the office behind the cash register and eventually the man left, pushing the door with his forearm and muttering under his breath. The rail official spoke out loud. He sounded apologetic. We have to be careful, he said. Last week one of them got into the ladies' toilet, she locked the door and sat in there screaming her head off the whole night.

It took us till two in the morning to get her out, we had to dismantle the cubicle.

I was looking at Tom. His neck muscles particularly, where they met the top of his shirt. We talked about how terrible it was that there were so many homeless people. No, it's scary, it's really scary, I said. I mean, that's one of the differences between now and then, isn't it? I don't really remember there ever being beggars on the streets, or anybody who needed money or asked for money like that, not when I was a child.

Mm, Tom said.

Except when my mother and I used to go through to Aberdeen on the train so she could go to Marks and Spencer's, I said. There was always an old man with one leg or one eye playing an accordion on the pavement. She always gave me something to put in the hat.

War-wounded, probably, Tom said.

In the sixties? I asked.

Yeah, probably, they'd still be around as late as the sixties, Tom said.

I used to feel like a rich girl in a story, I said, or like one of the children in the Mary Poppins film who gave the old woman money for feeding the birds. I used to be in my best clothes for going to Aberdeen. When I put it in the hat I actually used to feel like I was giving money to a different kind of human being from me.

Didn't you have a Marks and Spencer's where you lived? Tom asked.

Not until the eighties, I told him, and explained about the free buses they ran to and from all the highland villages when it came, so that people could come in to our town to the new shopping centre. I wanted him to know I was clever. Of course, I went on, the free buses meant that nobody in the villages shopped locally any more. So all the local stores closed down. And then the buses stopped being free, and people had to pay to go miles to do their shopping.

Right, Tom said, nodding. He had grown up in a London suburb; he had told me he loved it when I talked about my Brigadoon childhood. Hardly Brigadoon, I had said, my chin on his chest on our first Sunday afternoon. Where I lived never disappeared, it was there all the time. It even has a McDonalds now.

I'm starving, Tom said in the café while we were waiting for the train. He rocked in his chair and stretched his arms and shoulders. A woman at the next table looked at him.

But honestly, I said earnestly, knowing her eyes were on us. Don't you remember that feeling, that things were better and that there would be even better to come?

Tom looked blank.

And look at it now, I said. Look at us now. Look at that man who was in here. It's so hopeless. Now, soon, people aren't going to be able to afford to put their heating on. Or to get ill.

Well actually, Tom said, I don't remember any of that at all. I'm a different class, remember. You were aspiring in the sixties and seventies. We were much less well off than the others in the street we lived in. I mean we had a house and a car, but it was always a stretch for my father to keep them. We ate potatoes all the time. Sometimes there were hardly any Christmas presents.

Right, I said, right, yes, it's very different, isn't it?

Our train was announced with an apology for its late running. It was one of the new shuttle service trains, newly upholstered with prints of East Anglia screwed on to the walls. The first seat we sat in was broken so we moved to the next section of the carriage past the plastic wall. The train had moved off almost without us realising it was going, it was very smooth. It smells of sick in here, Tom said. After he'd said it I could smell it too, faint, sweet. We moved to the next compartment.

On the way to London we stopped in the dark and stood still; you couldn't see anything out of the windows and nothing happened for some time. A man further up the compartment began to kick the door he was standing next to. The driver's probably drunk, Tom said. After all, it's almost Christmas. The older woman in the smart coat opposite raised her eyebrows and smiled. I thought about the father of the girl who lived along the street from us when I was a child, he drove trains and he was always drunk, would come home on his bicycle with his cap set right back on his head and his face the colour of ripe tomato, his bicycle weaving all over the road. He was a nice man. He grew tomatoes in his greenhouse, and sweet peas and peas in pods on a trellis down his garden path. He lost his job before he got ill and died. I was about to tell Tom but for some reason I didn't want to. I don't know why, because that was one of the things we had in common, fathers out of work. Mine had lost his roofing business, seen it dwindle from thirty men working for him to nine then to two then to bankruptcy in the mid-eighties. Then his partner went off with the ladder and set up in competition to him. Tom's father had worked for a pharmaceutical company as a salesman until the company made half their sales staff redundant. Now he spent his time sailing round the edge of England in his boat, Tom had told me that every time he went home his father showed him a new videotape of sea and land.

Zoë and Richard lived in a big old house owned by Richard. They answered the door with their arms round each other. Richard shook my hand and Zoë gave Tom a hug; they looked pleased to see each other. She put her hand on my arm and said she was delighted.

I remember I thought she looked tired, but I don't know if I said anything back because as soon as I stepped inside the front door I couldn't help but look at the giant photograph. It took up most of the wall space ahead of us in their hall, the full-face picture of a teenage boy with long girlish blonde hair; it was about seven feet high and four feet across and it was lit up, as if there were electric lights wired round the inside of the frame. It lit the whole hall. I recognised the boy, a singer or film star, but I couldn't think who he was. The picture was huge. He was very beautiful.

All round the sitting-room, on the walls, propped on the mantelpiece, were pictures of the same gold-skinned boy. His hair was different lengths in different photographs. In one he was looking over the top of motorbike handlebars. In another he looked like he was asleep. In a line drawing framed above the fireplace the same face looked straight out at us on the sofa. I put my hand out to pick up my drink and found that the coasters were pictures of the boy too. Eventually I noticed that

118

there were photos of other people in among those on the mantelpiece, one was of Elizabeth Taylor when she was about
twenty.

When will supper be ready, Miss Smart? Richard asked Zoë.

Supper's almost ready now Mr Jackson, Zoë answered.
They smiled at each other.

Yes, we're a bit late, sorry about that, Tom said. The connection was slow at Stevenage, then the train stopped in the
middle of nowhere, with no explanation, for twenty minutes.

Just stopped! Zoë said.

Yes, for twenty minutes. Didn't move, Tom said.

So, Linda, did you ever get to meet Shirley MacLaine?
Richard asked me.

No, I said. I clinked the ice in my glass. I didn't know what
he was talking about.

Her biographies are published by your company, aren't
they? Zoë said.

Oh, yes, I think so, I said, but I only edit on their academic
list.

Right, said Richard.

We all laughed. Tom and Zoë talked about the people they
had known at university. Richard told me about the time he
met Salman Rushdie and the time he almost dated Debbie
Harry. There was a picture of her on the mantelpiece too.

Dated's the polite word for it, he said.

I laughed politely.

When I went upstairs in the light of the giant picture there
were more pictures of the yellow-haired beautiful boy. There
were photos of him framed all the way up the stairs, Richard

Free love

and Zoë had fixed them on a slant the way my father had
framed and hung the pictures of vintage cars that my mother
once cut out of a calendar. We had woken up on Christmas
morning and there they were, lining the stairs. We had thought
they were the ultimate in taste.

The boy's face was melancholy even when he was smiling,
he seemed to be looking miserably out of every picture of
himself and I realised that that's what was making the room
downstairs so sad. On the upstairs landing there were shots of
him at different ages; young and bullishly pretty, almost cheru-
bic, surrounded by other boys in one; teenage and handsome
on a horse in the next; in his early twenties, surprisingly seedy-
looking, with his jumper up over his mouth in the third. In all
of them the face was sultry, dark, serious. I pushed open the
bathroom door. Three black and white portraits above the
bath made it a bit like a hair salon. But I couldn't remember his
name, until Tom started to tease Zoë over the food about still
having what he called her river fixation.

Well come on Zo, what's it all about? It's a bit much, all this,
he said.

Zoë's eyes darkened. She looked at the food on her plate.
Richard looked sternly at Tom.

Admit it, Tom said, laughing, not noticing. You're still a
teenager, aren't you. That adolescent crush has gone just a bit
too far, become a kind of madness. It's a religion substitute.
Isn't it? I mean. Look at all this stuff. How do you get Richard
to put up with it? An addiction, isn't it?

A tear fell into Zoë's pasta. Richard put his fork down and
squared his shoulders at Tom.

You don't understand, do you? he said. So few people do. It was nothing to do with addiction, neither his life nor his death. He lived the purest sort of life. I'm not saying he didn't dabble a bit, who doesn't nowadays, I know I have. But I'd hardly call what I did an addiction. Nor what he was doing. It's perfectly obvious to anyone who knows, that his death was a mistake.

Tom looked confused. I had remembered who River Phoenix was by now; it was only a month or so after he had died and there were articles in all the weekend supplements about his double life. Are you mourning him? I asked. Is that why all the pictures are up?

We are mourning him, yes, Richard said. But we had these pictures up long before he died. This isn't about his death. Death doesn't even touch what we feel for him, actually.

River Phoenix is dead? Tom said.

It's one of the things that brought Richard and I together in the first place, Zoë said in a voice cracked with feeling. We both agreed, we both felt that River was a beautiful person.

And a truly great actor, Richard said.

When did he die? Tom said. What happened?

Zoë pushed her chair back and left the room. Tom watched her go. His face was stricken.

I know he's truly great, Richard said. Because when I see one of his films, when I'm sitting there in the cinema watching him in action, even when I'm watching him on the small screen, I get this feeling that I just don't have enough senses to cope with what I'm being given. Do you know what I mean? I sit there and I wish I had twice, three times as many eyes, eyes all over my body, I wish I had ears all over me, to be able to take it all in properly, the way it should be taken in.

Zoë came back blowing her nose on a pink tissue and crossed over to the other half of the room. She bent down behind the television and came back with a small square box, and on to the middle of the table between the salad dressing and the salt and pepper mills she gently emptied out lots of shiny plastic. Badges, discs of plastic with key-ring chains attached, tiny plastic frames, tumbled out. Fixed in all of them were photographs of River Phoenix at different stages of his life.

Zoë, are you all right? Tom said.

Zoë was arranging the things on the table. Look at these, she said. They're my favourite.

There were small moulded plastic structures with doors; she was standing them up and opening their doors. The dead star looked out from inside.

Zoë puts these together herself, Richard explained. We send them to hundreds of people. Hundreds of people want them, from all over the world. We don't charge much, just enough to cover the overheads.

We had a letter from Australia last week, Zoë said. We regularly get mail from all over the globe.

Last month, said Richard, we even had a letter from Poland. They're desperate for information there, and for the press cuttings or the videos or these pretty things. And we run the newsletter. *River Drift*. We have since, when was it, love? He even read it. We know because the management of the American fan club contacted us to wish us all the best. They said he had enjoyed it and sent his very best wishes.

September nineteen eighty-nine, said Zoë. She was looking less tearful now. She showed us the filing cabinet by the bookcase, half full of letters from subscribers and well-wishers, the other half full of pictures and articles. She showed us their shelves of video, their films and interviews and entertainment programmes and TV reports collected from all over the world.

No, we have reps in every country almost, recording things for us, Richard said. Of course, we've been tremendously, we've been tremendously busy since the end of October.

I still can't believe it, Zoë said. In another world than this, I still can't believe it.

I said they should call their newsletter *Off the Planet* now that he had gone to another world than this. Zoë wrote it down. Lots of people have suggested *Phoenix Rising*, as you would expect, she said, but we haven't made up our minds yet.

After supper Richard and Zoë left us to ourselves while they cleared up. I wanted to talk to Tom but he switched on the television almost at once. They had thirty channels on their TV and when Richard came through to put the liqueur glasses away he showed Tom how, if there was nothing on that particularly interested him, he could call the teletext pages up. We could check the stockmarket or read our horoscopes in Spanish. Or in German, French or Italian. We could find out what was in the charts twenty years ago tonight if we wanted.

Tom flicked through each channel silently. At last he settled on a show where viewers send in clips of themselves doing stupid things on home video and the TV company pays them if their clips are shown. A man was sitting at a table laid for a party but his chair was right next to the swimming-pool. Any moment now he was going to fall in. The studio audience was roaring with laughter. Tom pressed something and the screen was overlaid with words describing a court case where some people were being tried for torturing a girl. Before I had read the first paragraph the text changed again. Now it was about a couple from Liverpool who had spent five years secretly filming animal cruelty in Spain. There was going to be a documentary about them showing some of their film of bulls and cows being speared in front of a cheering crowd, and a goat being thrown off the top of a church steeple.

We could still see the video clip programme going on behind the words and hear the funny music and the audience. I read the whole report about the animals three times, and I wanted to find the writing about the girl's murder again. But when I asked Tom for the remote control he gave me a strange look, as if he were trying to tell me something important but couldn't say it because Richard and Zoë would overhear. He cleared the screen. Now on someone's home video three middle-aged women ran forward to catch the bouquet at a wedding, but they collided with each other and all fell over. The studio audience howled. I laughed too. I couldn't help it, it was funny.

Later, in the guest bedroom, Tom sat on the end of the bed with his head in his hands. Through the wall we could hear Richard and Zoë chatting and laughing. Tom sat stonily until I put my arms round him.

What a night, he said. What a horrific night. I can't believe how rude he was. I can't believe it.

He spoke under his breath. I sat back against the bedhead and let him talk.

Did you see how he ignored me? he said. How he cut me out of every conversation? Every question he asked was directed at you, Linda. Everything he said. Every time I spoke to Zo it was the same. Interruption, then change the subject, interruption, then change the subject. Christ! I didn't know people could be so childish.

I got up and stood by the window and looked out on to the wet street. Tom went on talking about how rude Richard had been.

I mean, I was perfectly ready to like him, he said. I was perfectly predisposed to like the man. But in a situation where someone's so blatantly rude! Did you see how many times I tried to start a conversation and he ignored me? There was no way Zo and I were going to get to talk to each other. The bastard. The bastard.

Eventually Tom went to have a shower. I didn't really want to undress or get ready for bed; I stood where I was, looking out of the window, and I saw a fox cross the road. I had known there were foxes in inner London, of course, I'd seen programmes about them, but this was the first time in my life that I'd ever seen a real one.

The fox was quite large, as large as a middle-sized dog; it slipped out of the front garden of the house directly opposite and crossed towards me. There was no traffic though you could hear the rest of London in the background. The fox didn't seem to be bothered by the noise. I watched it come coolly across the road, it stopped to sniff mid-air and to choose which way to go next and vanished off to the left of me, I watched it slip away directly below into the darkness between the plastic rubbish bins and the broken pillar at the front of the house next door.

When I looked round Tom was behind me, his hair was all wet and there was a towel round his shoulders. I put my arm round him and he caught my hand.

I sneaked back through for a kiss, he said, but he said it very loud. Then we kissed, and he made a satisfied sound. I'll be back for more in a minute, he said, and even his laugh was a little too loud. I laughed too.

So when Tom went back to the bathroom I picked up my jacket and went down the stairs. I shut the front door as quietly as possible and guessed my way back to the underground. It was very late but I wasn't as scared as I'd have imagined and once I found the main road it was easy.

It was cold and I wrapped my scarf so that it would cover my nose and mouth, and walked as if I were a boy the way one of my friends once showed me, that way people aren't as likely to attack you on the street. I looked steadily away from people on the underground platform and kept my eyes down on the tube and the pavement. On my way to the station all the rubbish from the shops had been put out for collection. I saw half-eaten burgers thrown away on the street. Nothing was open except an amusement arcade; I had to pass too close by a man in an anorak shouting obscenities at the bouncer who blocked the doorway of the arcade. The bouncer was pretending not to notice. Then I saw that the man was drooling, and that he was shouting into a portable radio he was holding next to his mouth. Little pools of his own saliva had formed at his feet.

I caught the last train out of the city that night, it would take me home direct and it left on time. It was a new train again, but with no heating in the carriage I was in. There was a tiny swastika carved carefully in the window by my head.

Over on the other side of the carriage was a woman in what looked like her fifties, maybe her forties. She sat beside a big torn rucksack, the canvas kind that climbers use, it had a wooden walking stick tied on to it. When she smiled at me I could see how the skin on her face had toughened. I watched her pick a piece of newspaper off the floor and try to read it. She gave up after a moment and instead she tucked it over her legs and under the sides of her coat. She smiled at me as she did this. She said, it's probably far too hot in the other carriages. We're better off here.

I smiled back and nodded and put on my headphones; I took out my favourite cassette, Brazil Classics 2, and read the sleevenotes before I put the box back in my bag. This music is a respectful prayer, they said, in honour of the sweet sensuous life-giving aspects of ourselves and our lives – and to the Earth, the mother of us all. To shake your rump is to be environ-mentally aware.

I put my feet on the seat opposite and closed my eyes. We were hurtling between small towns in the dark. I pushed my hands up inside my sleeves to keep them warm.

The unthinkable happens to people every day

I'm sorry son but there's no one of that name lives here.

The man hung up, stood in the phone box and breathed out slowly. Without warning London surrounded him, widening round him like rings in water with its scruffy paint-peeled shops, its streets leading into other insignificant streets, its anonymous houses for all the grey seeable distance. Someone rapped on the glass, a woman scowling from under her umbrella, and as he came out he saw people waiting in a line behind her. He crossed the road and stood outside a television shop with the sets in the windows showing one of the daytime programmes where two presenters and an expert discuss an issue and viewers phone in and talk about it. That was when he went inside the shop and within a few minutes had smashed several of the sets.

Now the man was driving too fast for his car, he could hear it rattling and straining under the tape of The Corries, the one tape that had been in the glove compartment when he looked. Above the noise there was a hum in his ears like when you wet your finger and run it round the rim of a glass. He thought that's what it had been like, like going into a room full of wine glasses. Nothing but wine glasses from one end of the floor to the other, imagine. As soon as you got into a room like that, he thought, the temptation to kick would be too strong. The same as when he was a boy and they visited the McGuinness's, when he was handed that china saucer and the cup with the fragile handle, with the lip of it so thin against his own that it would be really easy to bite through. As soon as a thought like that came into your head you wanted to try it. That ache in his arm to twitch suddenly and send the tea into the air. That would have made his folks laugh. They might have been cross to start with, but after that it'd have been something to remember.

He had stepped inside the TV shop to get out of the way of passers-by. Sleek new televisions were ranged in front of him, small ones on the top shelf, larger ones in the middle, massive wide-screen sets on the floor on metal stands. All except two were showing the same picture and the sound was turned up on one; he heard the presenter hurrying a caller off the air so as to bring the next person on. The woman he was hurrying had apparently just told them about a wasting disease her daughter aged nineteen had been diagnosed as having and the

130

bespectacled expert, presumably a doctor giving advice, was shaking his head dolefully at the camera. The presenter said, well thank you for that call Yvonne, we hope we've brought a little bit of comfort to you on that, and your daughter too, but now let's go over to Tom who's calling from Coventry, I believe he's just heard he's been found HIV positive, am I right, Tom? The maps on the screens flashed where Coventry was.

The man leaned forward and tipped the television in front of him off its shelf; it crashed on to the top of the television below it. Its screen fragmented and there was a small explosion as all the sets in the shop went blank. In the time it took the young woman serving another man in the video section to get to the door of the shop, he had launched a portable cassette radio through the screen of another set and sent a line of small televisions chained together hurtling one after the other simply by nudging the first.

I'm sorry, it couldn't be helped, was what the man said. The woman told her boss Mr Brewer this, and that before she had a chance to call for help or anything he was off and because she was so shocked she didn't see which way. What the woman didn't tell Mr Brewer was that actually the man had stood in the debris before he left and had slowly and carefully written down an address and a telephone number on one of the price display cards as he apologised. She had the piece of card folded in her back pocket and could feel it pressing against her as she spoke to Mr Brewer. Maybe the man hadn't given her his real address. That was something she didn't want to know. Maybe he had, though. That was what she didn't want Mr Brewer to know.

Side Two of The Corries ended again and the machine switched automatically back over to Side One. The last sign had flashed past before he'd had a chance to see where he was. In the middle years of his life, in the middle of a dark wood. He couldn't remember what that was from. In the middle lane of the motorway in the middle of the night. In a service station in the middle of nowhere in the middle of a cigarette. He held his coffee and stared out into the dark. He ought to phone his wife, they'd maybe be frantic. Or perhaps he could try the number again. There were three payphones by the exit. Think about just picking up the receiver, putting the coin in, pressing the number he knew the shape of like he knew the shape of his own hands, the telephone ringing there in the dark. But look at the time, he didn't want to wake anybody, that wouldn't do, and so he drained his coffee and headed back to the car.

At first light the road was so full of steep drops and sudden lifts that it was like being at sea; he had to travel most of it in second gear. It was light enough to read the word Scotland on the big rock as he passed. The Corries snapped near Pitlochry in the middle of the Skye Boat Song. Since Scotland is only a few hours long, it was about ten when he tried the number again, this time from a call box in sight of the house.

He lifted the receiver and pressed the numbers, he closed his eyes tightly and opened them again to try to get rid of the dizzy feeling. The garden, the walls, the door. The tree, much bigger. The lawn, the hedge. The next door. The whole block. The sky above it. The bus-shelter, the grass where the bus-shelter met the concrete, the little cracks in the edges of the kerb, different, the same. The same, but new houses had been built at the back where the field had been. The windows of the new houses, with their different kinds and colours of curtains. Even before the phone was answered, he knew.

No, I'm sorry. Look, is it not you that's phoned a few times already? I'm sorry, I can't help you there son. There's nobody of that name here.

I know, he said. I won't call again. I'm really sorry to have bothered you. I'm just being stupid.

After that it was random. Soon he was coasting the wet green carsick roads of the north; a little later he saw that the petrol he had bought in Edinburgh was almost gone. His car eventually ground to a halt on a gravelly back-road next to a small loch. The man wound down the window and as the sound of his car in his ears died away he heard water and birds. He opened the door and stood up. Further down the beach a child was crouched like a frog on the stones, her hair hanging; behind her was a big white-painted house converted into a roadside restaurant, closed for the season. A pockmarked sign on the roof of the house said HIELAN HAME, underneath in smaller letters BURGERS BAR-B-Q TRADITIONAL SCOTTISH FARE LICENSED. Behind this a mass of trees, behind them in the distance two mountains still with snow on the peaks, then the sky, empty.

The man walked across the stones and stood in the litter at the edge of the water. The car door hung open behind him, and the engine clicked as it cooled down. A bird sang in the grey air. Water seeped cold over the sides of his shoes.

It was the Easter holidays and the girl was out on the stones looking for insects or good skimmers. Sometimes if you turned a big stone over you could find slaters underneath, it depended how close to the water it was. The real name for slaters was woodlice. The girl had decided to collect insects for various experiments. She wanted to try racing them, she also wanted to try putting different kinds in a tupperware box together and to see which kinds survived when you left them in water. Last summer she had discovered tiny tunnels in the back garden and she had followed one to an ant colony in the manure heap. To see what would happen she had poured Domestos from the kitchen cupboard on to it. First a white scum had come and some ants had writhed in it, taking a long time to die. The others had gone mad, running in all directions, some carrying white egg-looking things bigger than themselves. They had set up another colony on the other side of the heap and for days she had watched them cleaning out their old place, lines of ants carrying the dead bodies away and leaving them in neat piles under one of the rosebushes. She was very sorry she had done that thing. This year she was going to be more scientific but kind as well, except to wasps. If they were stupid enough to go in the jam-jars and drown it was their own fault.

Here was a good flat stone. As she stood up to see how many skims it would have she saw the man who had left his car in the middle of the road walking into the loch. He sat down in the water about ten feet out. Then his top half fell backwards and he disappeared.

She ran along the bay to look for him; she heard a splash somewhere behind her and turned round. The man was sitting up in the water again. He looked about the same age as her uncle, and she watched him take some things out of his pocket and fiddle about with them. As she got closer she saw he was trying to light a wet cigarette.

Mister, excuse me, she said, but your car's in the middle of the road, people can't get by.

The man shook his hand away from himself so he wouldn't drip water down on to a match.

Excuse me Mister, but is it not a bit cold, the water? Anyway your matches are soaking – my mother's got a lighter. I know where it's kept.

The man looked embarrassed. He pulled himself to his feet unsteadily and wiped his hair back off his face, then stumbled back through the shallows. The girl watched the water running off him. She didn't know whether to call him Mister or Sir.

Are you drunk, Sir?

No, I'm not drunk, the man said smiling. Water from his clothes darkened the stones. How old are you then? he asked.

The girl kept her distance. I'm nine, she said. My mother says I'm not to talk to strangers.

Your mother's quite right. I've got a daughter your age. Her name's Fiona, the man said, looking at his feet and shivering.

I told you it was cold, said the girl. She twisted round to skim her stone.

I could show you how to skim stones, said the man.

I know how to skim stones, the girl said, giving him her most scornful look. She expertly pitched the stone against the

135

surface of the loch. The man scrabbled about at his feet to find himself a good stone and she stepped out of the range of the drips that flew off him when he threw.

Not as good as you, said the man. You're an expert right enough.

That's because I do it every day, said the girl so the man wouldn't feel too bad. I live here, so I can. Are you on holiday here? Where do you live? she asked.

The man went a funny colour. Then he said, well when I was your age I used to live not far from here.

You don't sound very Scottish, said the girl.

That's because I've lived in London for a long time, said the man.

The girl said she'd like to live in London, she'd been there once and seen all the places they show you on TV. When she grew up, she wanted to work for TV, maybe on programmes about animals. Then she asked the man did he know that Terry Wogan owned all those trees over there.

Does he? said the man.

Yes, and a Japanese man whose name she couldn't remember owned the land over there behind the loch.

Who owns the loch? the man asked.

Me, I do, said the girl. And my father owns the house and my mother runs the restaurant. Are you redundant? My uncle was made redundant.

The man told the girl that no, he wasn't redundant and that, believe it or not, he worked for television. Had she ever heard of the programme called The Unthinkable Happens To People Every Day? The girl said she thought her mother watched it.

Then she said suspiciously, I don't recognise you from off the TV.

No, said the man, I'm not *on* the TV. I work in the background. I do things like phone up the people who write to us and ask them to come on the show to talk about the unthinkable thing that's happened to them. Then I add up how much it'll cost for them to come, and decide how long they'll get to talk about it.

The girl had grown respectful and faintly excited about talking to someone who might work for TV. She couldn't tell whether the water running down the man's face was from his eyes or his hair. He looked very sad and she suddenly felt sorry for him even though he wasn't actually redundant. She decided to do something about it.

Would you like to come up on to the roof? she asked the man.

Would I what? he said.

Would you like to come up on to the roof and throw some stones? I know this really easy way to get up there, said the girl.

The man filled his wet jacket pockets with stones the girl selected. She showed him, springing up lightly, how to climb from the coalshed roof on to the extension. From there the man could heave himself after her up the drainpipe.

You have to be very quiet or my mother'll hear, said the girl. It's a wonderful view even on a day like today, isn't it?

Yes, the man whispered.

The girl pointed at the HIELAN HAME sign twenty feet away. She was obviously a good shot; the paint had been chipped in hundreds of small dents.

137

It's two points for big letters and five points for small ones. There's a special bonus if you can hit the c of Scottish, she said. But *your* arms are probably long enough so that you could even reach the loch from here if you wanted, she added hopefully.

Right, said the man. Taking a stone as big as his palm, he hurled it. They watched it soar in silence, then there was a distant splash as it hit the water.

Yes! cried the girl. Yes! You did it! Nobody's ever done that before. Nobody ever reached the loch before. She jumped up and down. The man looked surprised and then very pleased.

Anne-Marie! called her mother at the thumping. Anne-Marie, I've *told* you about that roof. Now get down here. If you're at that sign again you'll feel the back of my hand.

The girl led the man down off the roof, watching that he put his feet in all the right places. Her mother, angry at first at a stranger being up on her roof, was soon amazed and delighted to meet someone who worked on The Unthinkable Happens To People Every Day. She made him tea and a salad, apologising for the fact that the restaurant was closed and there wasn't anything grander, and she dried his suit off for him. He told her that he was sort of a local boy really, but that he'd lived in England for a while. She said she could spot it in his accent. Had he been up visiting his parents, then? No, they were both dead, both some years ago now. He'd been up for a drive and to look at the place again. She asked him how he'd got wet. He said he'd fallen into the loch. He filled his car from a tank of petrol in the garage and before he left he promised the girl that he'd get the autographs of some famous children's TV presenters for her when he got back to work.

Some weeks later a packet arrived addressed to the Hielan Hame. Inside was a thank you letter for the girl's mother and several photographs of celebrities all signed To Ann Marie with best wishes. The girl took them to school and showed them to all her friends. She didn't even mind that they'd spelled her name wrong.

These are from the man who hit the loch, she told her friends. He works for the TV and he's been up on our roof.

The world with love

On a day when it looks like rain and you're wandering between stations in a city you don't know very well, you meet a woman in the street whom you haven't seen for fifteen years, not since you were at school. She has three children with her, one of them is even quite old, nearly the age you were when you were both friends, a girl who looks so like her mother did then that you shake your heads at each other and laugh. You tell each other how well you both look, she asks you about your job, you ask her about her children, she tells you she's just bought a sweatshirt with the name of the city on it for her daughter (they're visiting for the day) but she's refusing to wear it and it cost nearly twenty pounds. Her daughter, thin and determined-looking, glares at you as if daring you to make any comment at all. She reminds you so much of the girl you knew that your head fills with the time she smashed someone's guitar by throwing it out of the art room window, and you remember she had a dog called Rex. You decide not to mention the guitar and ask after the dog instead. He died ten years ago, she tells you. Then neither of you is quite sure what to say next. You're about to say goodbye when she says to you out of the blue, God Sam, do you remember that time the Ark went mad?

For a moment you don't know what she's talking about and you picture the animals baying and barking, snarling at each other and at the different species round them, at fat Noah and his family trying to keep the noise down. Then it comes, of course it comes, God yes, you say, what a day, eh? and as you're walking along the road, late for your appointment, it all comes, it all comes flooding back.

The French teacher, the Ark everybody called her because her name was Mrs Flood. She liked you, she liked you especially, you were clever. She liked you so much that you hated her class, you hated it when she asked you, and she always did with that tone in her voice that meant, you won't disappoint me, you'll give me the answer, you'll know what it means, you'll know how to say it. The day she called you Sam instead of your full name in front of all your friends, like she was your friend or something, you were mortified, how dare she. How dare she single you out, how dare she make you seem clever in front of everybody, eventually you began to slip a few wrong answers in, and when you did the other girls had no excuse to give you a hard time afterwards.

Mrs Flood always talking about the beauty of French litera-ture with her singsongy highland island voice, scared of the tough mainland boys and the tough mainland girls, scared of your class even though you were the top stream, not much older than you herself really, her hair rolled up round her ears like the princess in Star Wars, her eyes like a shy rabbit, her plastic bangles on her wrist jangling into each other as she wrote beautiful French across the board in round letters, *Echo, parlant quant bruit on maine, Dessus rivière ou sus estan, Qui beauté eut trop plus qu'humaine*, pointing to the verbs with the pointer, *j'aurais voulu pleurer* she wrote, *mais je sentais mon coeur plus aride que le désert*, Sam, can you tell me the names for the tenses? she pleaded, and Sally Stewart's friend Donna poked you in the back and jeered in your ear, so it's *Sam* now is it, it's *Sam* now.

Do you remember the time the Ark went mad? The day you came into the classroom and sat down and got your books out as usual and she was standing at the window, staring out over the playing-fields, ignoring the noise level rising behind her as minute after minute passed, ten, fifteen, and each of you real-ising that it was as if she didn't even know you were there, she wasn't going to turn round, there wasn't going to be any French today. This was the day that one of the boys had brought in a ball of string and the people in the back rows began to tie all the desks at the back together, a network of string woven between the passageways. Somebody coughed out loud, then someone else made a rude noise and you all laughed in relief, but the Ark didn't move, didn't seem to hear. Then Sally Stewart crept out front and stood there like the teacher, you were all giggling, snorting with laughter, and still the Ark didn't turn round and Sally got braver and braver, touching, moving things around on the teacher's table.

She opened the big black dictionary in the middle, letting the cover hit the table with a crash. The Ark didn't look round, she didn't move, not even then, and Sally Stewart was flicking through it and then she was writing on the board the words *le pénis*, then *le testicule*, *les organes génitaux*, she got bolder, and in a teacher voice she said, I'm taking the class today since Mrs Flood isn't here. Who knows the word for to have it off? Who knows the word for french letters?

The boys were roaring, whistling, shouting, the girls were hissing high-pitched laughs, someone, you can't remember who, pulled the poster of the Eiffel Tower off the wall and it got passed round the class. You were laughing and laughing in that scared way and then you noticed that the new girl Laura Watt in front of you three along wasn't laughing, not at all, she was watching, her eyes were going back and fore from Sally at the board to the woman at the window, the Ark, the shoulderblades in her cardigan, her hands resting on the window-sill and her eyes watching a seagull gliding from the roof of the huts to the field. Laura Watt, the new girl, watching it all from behind her dark straight fringe, her chin on her hand, leaning on her elbow watching it. The girl who even though you hardly knew her had heard you say you liked a song and had made you a tape of the whole album, Kate Bush, *The Kick Inside*, and copied out all the songwords off the back of the sleeve for you in her nice handwriting, even though you hardly knew her, had hardly spoken to her. The paper with the words on it folded inside the tape box smelt strange, different, of what it must be like to be in her house or maybe her room, it was a scent you didn't want to lose so you found you were only letting yourself fold the pages open when you really needed to know what the songwords were.

Then Mrs Flood turned round and everything went quiet. Sally Stewart froze at the table with her hand on the dictionary, it was Sally Stewart who looked scared now, not Mrs Flood, who was laughing in a croaky way at the words on the board and who came across, cuffed Sally quite gently on the back of the head and gave her a push back to her seat.

Mrs Flood rolled the blackboard up and she read again what Sally had written on it. She added some accents to some e's, she put a chalk line through *les lettres françaises* and wrote above, the word *préservatif*. Then she pushed the board right up and wrote in large letters, bangles jangling in the silence, the words Look Upon The World With Love. Then she sat down at the table.

Write that down, she said, write it all down. Heads bent, you wrote it in your jotters, the words look upon the world with love, then you looked around at each other, and you carried on writing down the words on the board, the sex words Sally had found in the dictionary. You were writing until all of a sudden the Ark slammed the dictionary shut and said firmly, now, get out. Go on, she said when nobody moved, go on, off you go, get out, and slowly, unsurely, you all packed your books up and went, the people at the back had to pick their

145

way through the webs of string tied between the desks, and it wasn't until you were out in the corridor that you opened your eyes wide at your friends around you and you all made faces at each other as if to say God! and it wasn't until you were on the turn of the stairs that you let yourself say out loud God! what was all that about? and laughter broke out, and the whole class was clattering madly down the stairs, so noisy that the secretary came out of the headmaster's office to see what was happening and the class was rounded up and made to sit on the floor in the hall until it was time for the next period, and several of your friends were personally interviewed about it by the headmaster though you weren't. Mrs Flood was off school for three months and when she came back you didn't have her any more though you always smiled hello at her in the corridor even though she was obviously a weirdo. And remembering it all like this you can't help but remember what you had really forgotten, dark Laura Watt, and how once you even followed her home from school, keeping at a safe invisible distance on your racer, you watched her come to a house and go up a path and look in her pockets for a key and open the door and shut it behind her, you stood outside her house behind a hedge across the road for half an hour then you cycled home again, your heart in your throat.

Laura Watt, you had found you were thinking about her a lot. You scared yourself with how much you were thinking about her, and with how you were thinking about her. You thought of her with words that gave you an unnameable feeling at the bottom of your spine and deep in your guts. Because you couldn't even say them to yourself, you wrote lists of them in a notebook and you kept the notebook inside the Cluedo box under your bed. In case anyone were to find it you wrote the words FRENCH VOCABULARY on the cover and you filled it with words for the hands, the arms, the shoulders, the neck, the mouth. Words for the lips, the tongue, the fingers, the eyes, the eyes brown, the hair dark, the horse dark (a joke). Words you could only imagine, words like caresses, *les cuisses*. That word was enough to thrill you for three whole days, staring into space over your supper, your mother irritated, asking you what was the matter with you, you saying angrily, there is nothing at all the matter with me, your father and mother exchanging glances and being especially nice to you all that evening.

At night when everybody else was asleep you went through your pocket dictionary page by page from a to z and wrote in your notebook every word that might be relevant. *L'amie, l'amour, l'anarchie, l'anatomie, l'ange, être aux anges, anticiper.* Your French marks went up even higher, the new teacher, a nice Glaswegian girl who looked a bit like Nana Mouskouri, told you on the quiet (she understood these things) that you were the only person in the class who knew how to use the subjunctive. If it were to happen, she wrote on the board. You all copied it down, you watched the heads bent, the head bent three along and in front, you all copied down the words. If I were to say. If you were to see.

In the end you got the highest mark in the class and the only A for the exam in the whole school, you got the fifth year prize and you chose a copy of D. H. Lawrence's *The Virgin and the Gypsy* because it had naked people on the front and you and your friends thought it would be funny to see the Provost's face when he had to present you with it on prizegiving night. But on the night of the ceremony the Provost was a bit drunk, he mixed up the pages of his speech and he muddled the order of the prizes, when it was your turn to go up on stage with everybody clapping he gave you a book called *Sailing Small Yachts* and afterwards you had to go round like everybody else trying to find the right book and the owner of the book you'd been given.

Laura Watt was playing the violin at the prizegiving, she was top in music and was going to study it at university. One of the music teachers accompanied her on the piano and she played something by Mozart, you couldn't believe the quickness and slyness of her fingers on the strings and the way the music went through you like electricity, she was really good, everybody clapped, you clapped as loud as you could, you wanted to tell her afterwards, that was really great, you went up to her and she showed you the book the Provost had given her, it was *The Observer Book of Tropical Fish*. I don't have any tropical fish, she said, I chose an Agatha Christie novel. You both laughed, and you said to her, well done anyway, she was smiling, she said, well done yourself, you're awfully good at French, aren't you? You looked away to the side, shy and caught, you wanted to laugh or something, you said, yes, I am, I think.

Remember that, then, as you stop now, laughing into your hands in the rain, leaning against the wall of a grey office building in this beautiful city. Look around you in wonder again at where you are, remember the first night years ago when you went out with your prize book under your arm and her music still burning in your body, and all the walk home you saw the trees and how their branches met their leaves, the grass edging the pavement beneath your feet, the shabby lamp-posts reaching from the ground into the early night sky; you stopped and sat down where you were on the kerb between two parked cars, you knew the wheels, the smell of the oil, the drain full of litter next to you, the pitted surface of the road and the sky spread above you with its drifting cloud, and the words for every single thing you could sense around you in the world flashed through your head in another tongue, their undersides glinting like quicksilver.

LIKE

Ali Smith

'This endearing first novel' – *Elle*

'Beautifully written in precise, poetic prose that successfully evokes the love of like for like' – *Observer*

'I've thoroughly enjoyed the book, I love Ali Smith's prose – clear and lucid and at the same time full of little quirks and subtleties that makes hers an individual voice. Not only was the novel beautifully written but it was fascinating reading' – *Kate Atkinson*

There's Amy and there's Ash. There's ice and there's fire. There's England and there's Scotland. Ali Smith evokes the twin spirits of time and place in an extraordinarily powerful first novel which teases out the connections between people, the attractions, the ghostly repercussions. By turns funny, haunting and moving, *Like* soars across the hidden borders between cultures, countries, families, friends and lovers. Subtle and complex, it confounds expectations about fiction and truths. A seductive and exhilarating story of what it means to be alive at the edge of the twentieth century: here is a story of what it's like.

Now you can order superb titles directly from Virago